The Autumn of Terror

A Sherlock Holmes Adventure

The untold story series

The Autumn of Terror

The untold story of the Whitechapel Mystery

By Arthur Conan Doyle

A Sherlock Holmes Adventure

A novel by

Susith Ruwan

Truth is more dangerous than fiction.

Disclaimer:

All dates, places, events, details and people in this novel are historical, yet the story is a complete fiction written based on these historical facts.

There is no proof to verify any of the accusations made in this book, and the conclusion is purely based on creative interpretation, and not the truth.

This is a fiction written entirely for appreciation.

Susith Ruwan

The Map of Whitechapel 1888

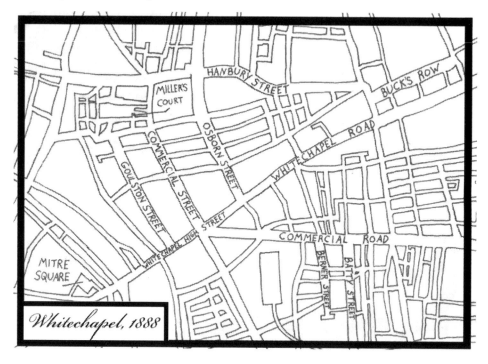

1.

"Whitechapel, again," I remarked, trying to engage my friend Holmes in conversation. Yet, he stood by the window, an unmoving sentinel against the grey London dawn.

I placed The Times upon the empty chair, the headline's stark declaration echoing in my mind. "Another dreadful murder, Holmes. The papers are rife with it. It seems Scotland Yard is baffled once more." I had perused the grim accounts of the murdered women in this morning's paper, hoping for some illuminating insight from my companion.

Holmes remained clad in the dressing gown he had worn the previous night, a clear indication that some matter had captured his attention since dawn and refused to release its hold upon his mind. I, therefore, forbore from chiding him for his silence, recognizing the signs of his deep contemplation. No doubt, some new problem was swirling within the labyrinthine corridors of his intellect, and I, warming myself by the fire, could see the glint of intellectual curiosity in his eyes.

"Scotland Yard seems to be floundering, Holmes," I remarked, hoping to nudge him towards this latest outrage. "This ghastly business in Whitechapel cries out for a mind such as yours." Indeed, the thought of these unsolved murders, these women slain in the fog-choked streets, filled me with a sense of urgency. I knew that if anyone could bring the perpetrator to justice, it would be my brilliant, if somewhat eccentric, friend.

He turned at last, his keen gaze piercing through the morning gloom. "And you, Watson, believe this latest tragedy to be the work of the same hand that has stained Whitechapel with blood these past weeks?"

"The brutality, the sheer callousness..." I shuddered, despite the comforting warmth of the fire. "Who else could it be?"

Holmes tapped his pipe against the mantelpiece, a wisp of acrid smoke curling upwards, momentarily obscuring his sharp features. "Motive, my dear Watson, is often a tangled skein. One must simply know where to seek the loose ends."

He fell silent, his gaze distant, and I knew better than to interrupt his deductions. His mind, a finely calibrated instrument, was already at work, dissecting the scant clues, piecing together the fragmented picture of the Whitechapel killer.

"You seem particularly engrossed in this case, Holmes," I ventured, hoping to draw him from his reverie. "More so than usual, I might venture."

A subtle smile touched the corners of his lips. "Perhaps, Watson. Perhaps. Tell me, what have you observed of my musings this morning?"

His question, though seemingly innocuous, held a familiar challenge. He delighted in testing my own powers of observation, however rudimentary they might be compared to his own. I recounted the subtle cues I had noted – his stillness, the intensity of his gaze, the lingering aroma of tobacco that spoke of a morning spent in deep contemplation.

"The street below, Watson," he interjected, his voice taking on a sharper edge. "The ceaseless flow of life outside our window. Tell me, what do you see?"

From his vantage point by the window from where he resided at 221/B, he commanded a clear view of Baker Street, bustling with its usual morning tide of pedestrians and hansom cabs.

I glanced out at the bustling thoroughfare. "Workers, clerks, shopkeepers, the usual morning throng."

"And yet," Holmes countered, his eyes fixed on the clock ticking steadily above the mantelpiece, "if we were to step out onto Baker

Street this very moment, could we glean a single clue about those who passed by just half an hour ago?"

"Footprints, perhaps?" I offered, grasping at straws. "Discarded items, a dropped handkerchief..."

He shook his head, a hint of disappointment in his expression. "Ephemeral traces, Watson, easily erased by the relentless tide of time. No, the past leaves its mark, but it is a subtle one, requiring a keen eye and a sharper mind to decipher."

I studied Holmes, noting the uncharacteristic dejection in his tone. It was clear this was no mere passing observation, but a thought that had been troubling him for some time. "Holmes," I inquired, "why does this matter so much?" He turned from the window, his movements abrupt, and rose to his feet.

His gaze shifted abruptly to the door. "Give me your chair by the fire, Watson. We are about to have a visitor."

He settled into the chair with a sigh, his gaze fixed on the door. I moved towards the window, a sense of anticipation quickening my pulse. Holmes's pronouncements were rarely wrong, and his demeanor suggested that this visitor was no ordinary caller.

A sharp rap on the door confirmed his prediction. As I turned the handle, a familiar face greeted me, a look of urgency etched upon his features.

2.

The face was familiar, yet I could not place it. I was certain we had crossed paths before, but the circumstances eluded me. The visitor was a man of obvious means, his attire impeccable – a finely tailored coat, a hat of the highest quality. There was not a wrinkle nor a speck of dust upon him.

I ushered him in, and he acknowledged me with a courteous nod before addressing my companion. "Mr. Holmes, I must apologize for this unannounced intrusion." His gaze went directly to Holmes, who remained seated by the fire, his expression unreadable.

A moment of silence hung in the air, and the visitor, sensing Holmes's expectation, cast his eyes downward before meeting my companion's gaze once more. "I was at a loss, sir," he continued, his voice carrying a note of both sincerity and distress. "And I must again apologize for neglecting the common courtesies of a morning call."

"A prominent Freemason," remarked Holmes, gesturing towards the empty chair opposite him, "would not seek me out at such an early hour without grave cause."

I confess, I was startled. How Holmes had deduced the man's affiliation with the Masonic Order, I could not fathom. Yet, our visitor seemed neither surprised nor offended by the revelation.

"Your reputation precedes you, Mr. Holmes," he replied, bowing slightly as he took the proffered seat. "London has presented you with a challenge worthy of your renowned talents. I am here to implore you to accept it."

My knowledge of the Freemasons was limited, gleaned from whispers and rumors that painted them as a shadowy, clandestine society. I found it difficult to reconcile this image with the impeccably dressed gentleman before us. Indeed, no other visitor to our humble abode had presented himself with such an air of refinement, not even the illustrious Prince of Bohemia himself.

Our guest, though outwardly composed, betrayed a certain restlessness in his eyes. "I am not surprised, Mr. Holmes, that you have identified my Masonic affiliation," he stated, his voice calm yet firm. "However, I assure you, it has no bearing on the matter at hand. Allow me to introduce myself. I am George Lusk, an architect by profession. I come to you, sir, as a concerned citizen of Whitechapel, to request your assistance in a matter of grave urgency. I trust you are already acquainted with the recent unfortunate events in our district." His words were measured, his tone conveying both authority and a deep sense of responsibility.

Holmes, drawing thoughtfully on his pipe, met Lusk's gaze directly. "And what, pray tell, is a Freemason's interest in these murders?"

Lusk remained unperturbed. "I reiterate, sir, my membership in that organization is entirely irrelevant. I have volunteered my services as a community leader, compelled by a sense of duty to protect my fellow citizens." His sincerity was evident in both his expression and his tone.

"It is an honor to make your acquaintance, Mr. Lusk," I interjected, extending my hand. He rose to shake it, his grip firm and reassuring.

Holmes, however, remained seated, puffing contemplatively on his pipe. With a subtle gesture, he indicated that Lusk should resume his seat. I retreated discreetly, sensing that my companion was about to deliver a pronouncement.

"I regret to inform you, Mr. Lusk," Holmes declared, "that I see no need to exert my faculties on this particular case. These murders bear the hallmarks of gang violence, a struggle for dominance in the seedy underbelly of Whitechapel. The local constabulary should be quite capable of handling such matters, provided they are properly motivated." He paused, his gaze fixed on Lusk. "And you, sir, strike me as a man who could provide the necessary encouragement."

Holmes leaned forward, his voice taking on a sharper edge. "Advise them to focus their attention on the gangs who prey upon the unfortunate women of the streets, extorting protection money. The victims, I suspect, are those who have refused to pay." He dismissed Lusk with a curt nod. "Inform the Inspector in charge. That will be all."

Lusk, however, remained rooted to his chair. He had clearly anticipated a different response, and a shadow of disappointment crossed his face. Leaning forward, he met Holmes's gaze with unwavering intensity. "Might I inquire as to the basis of your conclusion, Mr. Holmes?" he asked, his voice betraying no hint of agitation.

Holmes's reply confirmed my suspicion that he had been perusing the morning papers before my arrival. "The unfortunate woman found murdered on Brick Lane, near the Osborne Street junction – Emma Elizabeth Smith, I believe – resided in a public house on George Street, a mere stone's throw from the scene of the crime. Those who would threaten a woman of her profession in such close proximity to her lodgings would undoubtedly be familiar with her habits and her daily routine."

Lusk nodded slowly, his expression thoughtful. Even the most desperate of criminals, it seemed, sought to profit from the plight of these unfortunate women. "Indeed," he agreed. "The nature of her wounds, the manner in which she was... accosted, suggests robbery as well."

I realized then that Lusk was no mere concerned citizen. He possessed a keen intellect, a mind capable of grasping the intricacies of a criminal investigation.

"It appears," continued Holmes, "that this gang seeks to exert control over the, shall we say, 'unfortunates' of the East End. Or perhaps," he added, a speculative glint in his eye, "she was the victim of her own procurer."

Lusk removed his hat, placing it upon his knee. It was clear that this line of inquiry was not the true purpose of his visit.

"The other victim," Holmes went on, "Martha Tabram, also resided in a public house on George Street. She was murdered in the early hours of the morning, her body discovered in George Yard. The sheer number of wounds inflicted upon her – thirty-nine, I believe

– suggests a crime of passion, a frenzied attack fueled by rage. A broken romance, perhaps, or a rejected suitor."

Lusk absorbed this information, his brow furrowed in thought. The initial concern that had brought him to Baker Street seemed to have given way to a deeper, more perplexing dilemma.

My own curiosity, however, was piqued by a different detail. "Holmes," I interjected, "how did you know Mr. Lusk was a Freemason the moment he entered the room?"

Holmes glanced at our guest, a silent query passing between them. Lusk, with a slight inclination of his head, granted permission. It was evident, however, that his mind was preoccupied with a far weightier matter than the disclosure of his Masonic ties. My own memory offered no clue as to how Holmes had arrived at his deduction, and I felt compelled to seek enlightenment. "Holmes," I inquired, "how did you know?"

It seemed to me that Holmes, in his usual fashion, had already devoured the morning papers, dissected the Whitechapel murders, and laid bare the culprits before Lusk even crossed our threshold. The eagerness in his voice as he addressed my query confirmed my suspicions.

A hint of pride flickered in my companion's eyes. "My dear Watson, I invite you to examine Mr. Lusk's coat. Observe the pin adorning the collar of his shirt. Do you see the symbol engraved upon it? A capital 'G', surrounded by the tools of a builder – the square and compass. These, my friend, are the unmistakable emblems of the Masonic Order. The 'G', of course, represents Geometry, a cornerstone of their craft."

Lusk, crossing his legs, turned towards me with a wry smile. "There is, however, a more direct method of ascertaining a man's Masonic affiliation."

"And that would be?" I asked, intrigued.

"Simply to inquire," he replied, his tone matter-of-fact.

He produced a card from his waistcoat pocket and presented it to Holmes. I leaned in, attempting to decipher the inscription, but Lusk's gaze, sharp and authoritative, held me at bay.

Holmes, upon reading the card, raised his eyebrows in a gesture of mild surprise.

"You were correct in your deduction, Mr. Holmes," Lusk conceded. "However, one must remember that the mere possession of a symbol does not guarantee authenticity. I could have easily procured this pin through less than legitimate means. Direct inquiry, as I said, is the most reliable method."

Holmes nodded, acknowledging the point.

"Furthermore," Lusk continued, "a Freemason is under no obligation to reveal his membership. It is a matter of personal discretion. I, for one, make no secret of my affiliation. However," he added, displaying three rings upon his fingers, each bearing the Masonic emblem, "it is a subject rarely broached in casual conversation. This steel ring," he explained, indicating one of the three, "I acquired during my service in the Afghan War."

"I too served in Afghanistan," I interjected, eager to share a common experience.

Lusk, however, continued his discourse, seemingly oblivious to my remark. "The other two rings, along with this collar pin, are family heirlooms, passed down from my grandfather." He gestured towards a pair of cufflinks, also adorned with the Masonic symbol. "These I reserve for special occasions."

"The Freemasons are a private organization," he concluded, his tone regaining its initial gravity. "Therefore, do not assume that all members are as forthcoming as myself. Discretion is often the rule, and a man's membership is best revealed by his own volition."

"I understand, Mr. Holmes," Lusk said, his voice carrying a hint of weariness, "that the reputation of my fraternity precedes me. Rest assured, however, that the matter at hand has no connection to the Masonic Order. I give you my word as a gentleman."

I felt a pang of shame at my own unfounded suspicions. This was clearly a man of integrity and intellect, one who held himself to a higher standard than most. His openness about his Masonic affiliation, evidenced by the numerous symbols adorning his person, spoke volumes of his character.

Holmes, with a subtle gesture, passed me Lusk's calling card. I took it and moved towards the window, settling into the chair my companion had recently vacated. The card, engraved in a crisp, professional font, read:

GEORGE LUSK,
BUILDER & DECORATOR,

BRICKLAYER, PLASTERER, CARPENTER PLUMBER, PAINTER, GASFITTER,
AND CONTRACTOR FOR GENERAL REPAIRS.

ROOFS AND DRAINS PROMPTLY ATTENDED TO
SANITARY WORK A SPECIALITY.

THE CHEAPEST HOUSE IN THE TRADE.
HOUSE, ESTATE, AND GENERAL INSURANCE AGENT.
RENTS COLLECTED AND ESTATES MANAGED.

PLEASE NOTE THE ADDRESS :—

ALDERNEY ROAD. GLOBE ROAD
MILE END. E,

Lusk, with a measured grace, rose from his chair, his hand briefly touching his chest in a gesture of respect. He leaned lightly upon his cane, not out of necessity, I surmised, but as a mark of distinction, or perhaps a subconscious need for reassurance. He was a man of robust physique, his strong features framed by a neatly trimmed moustache, yet there was a tension in his stance, a hint of unease that belied his outward composure.

As he turned to depart, Holmes and I exchanged a knowing glance. We had misjudged our visitor, dismissing his concerns too readily.

"Mr. Lusk," Holmes said, rising swiftly from his chair, "I sense that we have not fully grasped the nature of your request. Pray, enlighten us as to your expectations. We are all ears."

I knew that nothing troubled my friend more than an unsolved puzzle, a secret left unrevealed.

"I am not a man easily given to anger," Lusk replied, his voice controlled, though I noticed Holmes's gaze lingering upon the hand that gripped the cane with a force that suggested suppressed agitation. "However, I have not yet had the opportunity to fully explain the purpose of my visit."

"Please, be seated," Holmes urged, his tone unusually deferential. Lusk hesitated for a moment, then resumed his chair, placing his hat upon his lap and leaning his cane against the wall. With deliberate care, he removed his gloves, folding them neatly within the crown of his hat. He sat ramrod straight, his gaze fixed upon Holmes, awaiting a signal to proceed.

Holmes, sensing his readiness, withdrew his pipe from his lips and gestured with it. "Pray, continue, Mr. Lusk."

My companion settled back in his chair, prepared for a lengthy narrative. Lusk, however, remained rigidly upright, his posture suggesting a man accustomed to bearing a heavy burden. I, perched upon the edge of my seat by the window, leaned forward, eager to catch every word.

Lusk gestured towards the newspaper lying upon the teapoy. "These recent murders, Mr. Holmes," he began, his voice low and measured, "are but the latest in a series of tragedies that have befallen our district. However, to delve into the past would only serve to cloud the issue. I shall, therefore, confine my account to the events of this very morning." His gaze locked with Holmes's, a silent plea for understanding in his eyes.

"This morning!" I exclaimed, rising from my chair in astonishment. Holmes, too, betrayed his surprise, the pipe momentarily forgotten as it slipped from his grasp. Surely, if a murder had occurred mere hours ago, our presence at the scene would be imperative. Yet, Lusk remained unperturbed.

"While the immediacy of the event is undeniable," he replied calmly, "there is, alas, no need for haste. The deed is done. However, this killer must be stopped, and I have been led to believe that you, Mr. Sherlock Holmes, are the man for the task. Allow me to present the facts as I know them, and then, sir, you may decide whether to lend your considerable talents to this most urgent of matters."

He paused, awaiting Holmes's response. My companion, however, remained silent, drawing deeply on his pipe until the last wisp of smoke had dissipated.

"Proceed, Mr. Lusk," Holmes said at last, recognizing that our visitor would not be swayed from his methodical approach.

Lusk, his voice now taking on the measured cadence of a formal report, began his account. "This morning, on the thirty-first of August, another horrific murder has stained the streets of Whitechapel. However, this crime differs markedly from its predecessors. The motive, the identity of the perpetrator, the very nature of the act itself, remain shrouded in mystery."

"At a quarter to four this morning," he continued, "Constable Neil, badge number 97J, was making his rounds on Bucks Row, the street adjacent to the London Hospital. He discovered a woman lying upon the pavement, apparently in a state of inebriation. Upon attempting to assist her, he discovered, to his horror, that her throat had been savagely cut. A closer examination revealed a multitude of other wounds, any one of which could have proved fatal."

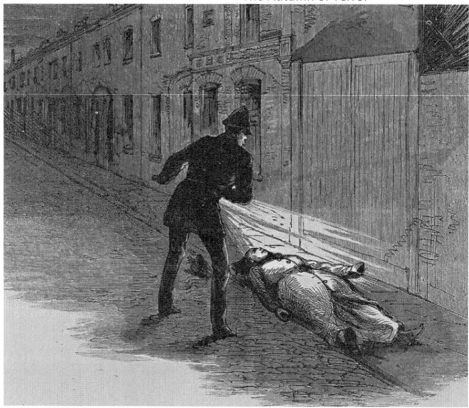

Holmes sprang from his chair, his movements as swift and decisive as a striking cobra. "We must go at once, Watson! The scene must be secured before any vital evidence is disturbed."

"I anticipated your eagerness, Mr. Holmes," Lusk replied, rising with unruffled composure. "I took the liberty of requesting the Inspector in charge to preserve the scene until your arrival."

"Then we must not tarry a moment longer," declared Holmes, turning to me with that familiar glint in his eye that signaled the start of a new adventure. I nodded, my own pulse quickening with anticipation.

"Excellent!" exclaimed Lusk. "My carriage awaits below."

Holmes, shedding his dressing gown, donned his coat and deerstalker cap with characteristic speed. "Come, Watson," he said, his voice charged with a grim determination. "We have an autumn of terror to bring to an end."

3.

Lusk's carriage conveyed us swiftly yet safely through the labyrinthine streets of Whitechapel. I deduced that our driver had received prior instructions, for Lusk uttered not a word to him throughout the journey. We arrived at our destination mere minutes before nine, the morning air thick with a chilling blend of fog and anticipation.

A lone constable stood guard, his figure stiff and unmoving. As we alighted from the carriage, however, another officer came rushing towards us, his breath ragged and his face flushed with exertion.

"I waited, sir," he gasped, struggling to regain his composure, "until the ambulance arrived from Bethnal Green and conveyed the body away."

The gleaming badge upon his lapel, bearing the number 97J, identified him as Constable Neil, the officer who had discovered the unfortunate victim.

"My apologies, Mr. Lusk," he said, his voice laced with regret. "We received explicit orders from the Mayor to remove the body without delay. It has been transported to the Montague Mortuary."

"A most unfortunate decision," Holmes remarked, his tone laced with displeasure. "The removal of the body before a thorough examination of the scene has undoubtedly compromised our investigation. Vital clues may have been lost."

"We understand your concerns, sir," the constable replied, his gaze shifting between Lusk and Holmes, "but we are bound to obey the Mayor's directives."

"I comprehend the Mayor's predicament," I interjected. "The sight of an unidentified female corpse lying exposed upon the street would hardly inspire confidence in the citizenry."

Lusk turned to Holmes, a hint of frustration in his voice. "What course of action do you suggest, Mr. Holmes?"

"Constable Neil," Holmes said, addressing the weary officer, "you have endured a most trying morning. Return to your station, take a hearty breakfast, and endeavor to get some rest. We shall summon you if your assistance is required. You have our gratitude for your service."

"Appetite, sir, is a luxury I fear I cannot afford at present," replied Constable Neil, with a wan smile and a nod of farewell, before turning to retrace his steps.

Holmes surveyed the scene, his brow furrowed in frustration. The premature removal of the body had dealt a blow to his investigative process, of that there was no doubt. "Ensure this area remains undisturbed until our return," he instructed the remaining constable, his tone brooking no argument.

Without further ado, he climbed into the waiting carriage and barked, "Montague Mortuary!" Lusk and I lingered on the pavement, momentarily taken aback by his abruptness. The driver, too, seemed startled by Holmes's peremptory command, but a calming gesture from Lusk allayed his concerns.

Lusk drew the constable aside, engaging him in a hushed conversation. The officer, initially eyeing Holmes with a mixture of curiosity and resentment, seemed to relax as Lusk spoke, his demeanor shifting from suspicion to deference.

"Rest assured, Watson," Lusk said, rejoining me with his usual composure, "this location will be guarded until our return." His words, though directed at me, were clearly intended for Holmes's ears as well.

He followed me into the carriage, and with a tap upon the roof, we set off once more. Our pace, however, was markedly slower than our initial journey, a testament to Lusk's methodical nature, a stark contrast to the whirlwind of energy that was my friend, Sherlock Holmes.

4.

Upon arriving at the mortuary, Lusk's influence granted us immediate access to the deceased.

"We've endeavored to ascertain her identity, sir," the mortuary attendant explained to Lusk, "but thus far, our efforts have proved fruitless."

Lusk performed the necessary introductions, then stepped back, allowing Holmes to take center stage.

We approached the body, laid out upon a cold, steel table, and began our examination.

She was a woman of unremarkable appearance – five feet in height, perhaps forty years of age, with a plain face framed by dark, curly hair. Her eyes, now forever closed, were a dull blue, and her clothing was of the common sort. I was not surprised that she remained unidentified. She was, alas, a typical denizen of these impoverished streets, easily lost in the teeming masses of Whitechapel.

Holmes commenced his examination, his long fingers gently probing the cold flesh. At his invitation, I joined him, my medical training lending a different perspective to the grim task.

Lusk, perched uncomfortably upon a narrow bench, watched our every move, his cane held firmly in his grasp. The mortuary attendant, a stoic man with eyes that had seen too much, stood beside him, his gaze fixed upon the body, a silent testament to the horrors that unfolded within these walls.

We noted the missing teeth in the lower jaw, the tongue bearing the marks of a desperate bite, a bruise upon the right jawline. "Thumb pressure, rather than a fist," Holmes murmured, indicating the mark for my inspection. I nodded, a chill creeping down my spine despite the stifling air of the mortuary.

Her nose, large and prominent, was a distraction from the true horror that lay upon her neck. A gaping wound, four inches in length, ran from beneath her left ear, a cruel parody of a smile. Below it, a deeper incision, eight inches long, circled her throat, severing the delicate tissues, exposing the very vertebrae beneath.

The arteries and veins on both sides had been severed with surgical precision.

As a physician, I was struck by the clinical nature of the wounds, the methodical savagery that had been employed. It was as if a skilled surgeon had wielded the blade, not a frenzied madman. A shiver ran through me, and I found myself averting my gaze from the ghastly spectacle.

The lack of blood upon her chest and clothing was perplexing. The carnage was confined to her neck and abdomen, where a series of deep slashes had ripped through flesh and muscle, exposing the organs within.

"Each incision made from left to right," Holmes observed, miming the action with his own left hand. "Our killer, it seems, is left-handed."

He turned his attention to her clothing, carefully examining each garment. From a pocket, he retrieved a comb and a small, cracked mirror, holding them up for our inspection before setting them aside. With the assistance of the mortuary attendant and myself, he removed the remaining clothes, revealing the full extent of the brutality inflicted upon her.

For a time, he stood in silent contemplation, his gaze fixed upon the naked body. Then, with a sigh, he turned his attention to the discarded garments, his magnifying glass held aloft. I took a seat beside Lusk, allowing Holmes to pursue his investigation undisturbed.

After a meticulous examination of the garments, Holmes laid them upon the table, his magnifying glass hovering over them like a hawk circling its prey. "Gentlemen," he announced, approaching us with a piece of underclothing in hand, "I believe we have a means of identifying our unfortunate victim."

We rose from our seats, the mortuary attendant stepping forward with a look of morbid curiosity.

Holmes held aloft the undergarment, a simple chemise. "Mr. Lusk," he said, "your knowledge of this district is extensive. Can you make anything of this?"

Lusk recoiled slightly, a flicker of disgust crossing his features. The constable, too, grimaced at the sight of the stained garment. I craned my neck, attempting to discern the nature of the mark.

Holmes offered his magnifying glass to Lusk, who declined with a shake of his head. He leaned forward, peering intently at the stain. I followed suit, my own curiosity piqued.

Emblazoned upon the fabric was a symbol, a series of letters intertwined in a distinctive pattern.

"There appears to be a stencil mark," Holmes observed, holding the garment steady for Lusk's inspection. "Do you recognize it?"

"Lambeth Workhouse," Lusk replied, his voice low and grave.

"The emblem of the Lambeth Girls' House!" exclaimed the constable, bending closer for a better view.

"Precisely," said Holmes, a gleam of satisfaction in his eye. "Dispatch a team to the public houses in the vicinity, constable. Someone there will surely recognize her. And send two more officers to fetch the matron of the Lambeth Girls' House. She may be able to provide a positive identification."

"Public houses, Mr. Holmes?" Lusk inquired, his tone laced with a hint of reproach. "Are you suggesting this poor woman frequented such establishments?"

"The comb and mirror found in her pocket, Mr. Lusk," Holmes replied, "were well-worn, suggesting a certain familiarity with the amenities offered by such establishments."

Lusk and the constable exchanged a glance, a silent acknowledgment of Holmes's deduction. Orders were swiftly issued, and officers dispatched to pursue the leads.

"Now, gentlemen," Holmes declared, his voice brisk and businesslike, "let us return to the scene of the crime. With any luck, the killer has left us some trace of his presence."

5.

Upon our return to Bucks Row, we found the constable still diligently guarding the scene. There was no mistaking our destination.

A handful of other officers lingered nearby, their demeanour suggesting a casual indifference that struck me as rather unprofessional.

As we approached, I observed Holmes's keen gaze sweeping over the surroundings, taking in every detail, his attention momentarily lingering upon two of the loitering constables. I attempted to follow his line of sight, knowing that his powers of observation far exceeded my own. He saw things, I knew, that remained hidden to the untrained eye. The street itself was unremarkable – a row of respectable houses on one side, a high, impenetrable wall flanking the other.

Lusk, with a subtle gesture, dismissed the constable guarding the scene. The officer approached us, his expression a mixture of curiosity and deference.

"Mr. Holmes," he said, his voice somber, "I regret that I cannot offer you a pleasant good morning. This unfortunate affair is now in your capable hands. Mr. Lusk has placed his trust in you, and we are at your disposal. You are, of course, aware that two similar murders have occurred in the past year."

Holmes merely nodded, his expression unreadable. He clasped his hands behind his back and surveyed the scene, his gaze sharp and predatory, like a hawk circling its quarry. Suddenly, he stooped, his magnifying glass appearing as if by magic, focusing upon a point on the cobblestones.

Lusk and the constable exchanged a startled glance, but I remained unfazed. I had witnessed this behaviour countless times before, and knew it to be a sign that Holmes's mind was fully engaged.

I, too, surveyed the street, attempting to view it through the eyes of a killer. It seemed an unlikely location for such a brutal act, exposed and open to view. "What would compel a murderer to choose such a public place?" I wondered aloud.

Holmes, having scrutinized every inch of the ground, rose to his feet, his expression one of disappointment. He began to pace restlessly up and down Bucks Row, his mind clearly grappling with the lack of obvious clues.

Lusk and the constable, their attention now drawn to me, awaited my response.

"Bucks Row, sir, is a street of respectable residences," the constable offered, gesturing towards the well-maintained houses. "Gentlemen of means, not the sort to be involved in such savagery." He then indicated the imposing wall that ran along the opposite side. "And as you can see, sir, the other side is entirely impassable, blocked by this wall, which runs the length of the street, bordering the warehouse beyond."

"Indeed," added Lusk, "access is limited to either end of Bucks Row."

"Therefore," I concluded, perhaps stating the obvious, a habit for which Holmes often chided me, "the perpetrator must have entered from one of those two points."

At that moment, Holmes strode towards us, his brow creased in thought. "There is nothing of value here, gentlemen," he declared, his tone laced with disappointment. "As I suggested to Mr. Lusk, these murders bear the hallmarks of gang violence, likely those ruffians who prey upon the unfortunate women of the night, demanding protection money." He turned to the constable. "Have you received any reports of such activity?"

24

The constable nodded, a flicker of hesitation in his eyes. "Indeed, sir. There have been instances of these, ahem, 'unfortunate women' being accosted by such thugs, particularly those who refuse to comply with their demands." He seemed unable to utter the word "prostitutes," a testament, I thought, to his decent upbringing.

"This latest tragedy," he continued, "could well be another such incident."

His words, however, were met with a shared look of disbelief from both Lusk and Holmes.

"Another murder occurred just last month, on the sixth of August," Lusk interjected. "The victim, also stabbed, was discovered in the gutter, surrounded by a pool of blood."

"And yet," Holmes countered, "I find no such evidence here. I have examined every inch of this street, and there is not a single trace of blood, nor any other clue that might lead us to the perpetrator."

Lusk nodded grimly.

"It seems highly improbable that the murder occurred here," Holmes continued, his voice taking on a thoughtful tone. "Surely, her screams would have roused the entire neighbourhood. Yet, no one has reported hearing any disturbance."

"Aside from the usual detritus one finds upon the pavement," Holmes observed, "there is not a single trace of disturbed earth. This, Mr. Lusk, is significant."

"You believe she was not murdered here?" Lusk inquired, his brow furrowed.

"It is inconceivable, sir," Holmes declared, his voice rising in agitation. "Had she been slain upon this spot, there would be a veritable pool of blood. The evidence would be undeniable!"

At that moment, the constable, forgetting our presence, leaned towards Lusk, whispering something in his ear.

"Constable," Holmes interjected, his tone sharp with disapproval, "if you insist on conducting clandestine conversations, we shall be forced to withdraw our assistance. We are here to aid in your investigation, but we require your full cooperation, including the sharing of all pertinent information, however insignificant it may seem."

Lusk, sensing Holmes's displeasure, gestured for the constable to speak freely.

The officer's face grew somber.

"Upon discovering the body, Constable Neil immediately summoned Dr. Llewellyn to confirm the, ahem, unfortunate woman's demise. Constable Neil, as you gentlemen witnessed, was understandably shaken by the experience," the officer continued. "He was, after all, the one who discovered the poor woman during his rounds on Bucks Row. You saw his state when he handed over the watch to me. Therefore, I feel it is my duty to relay what he confided in me while we awaited your arrival. I am certain he would not object."

The officer leaned closer, his voice dropping to a conspiratorial whisper. "He immediately dispatched a cab to alert the station, and another to summon a doctor. It was Dr. Llewellyn who arrived first, his surgery being less than three hundred yards from the spot where the body was found." He pointed towards a nearby street.

We all followed his gesture, our gazes drawn to the building he indicated.

"The doctor, roused from his slumber, arrived hastily, and proceeded to examine the body where it lay, upon which he remarked the very same discrepancy. 'Where is the blood?' he inquired. 'One would expect a veritable pool, given the nature of her wounds. Has a vampire been at work?'"

I recalled the small patch of blood we had seen upon our arrival, hastily scrubbed away by the constables before our departure.

Holmes, too, had noted this detail, and a look of annoyance crossed his face. However, he remained silent, allowing Lusk's carriage to convey us onwards.

6.

Despite the constable's chilling account, I found my thoughts drifting towards fanciful tales of blood-sucking killers. However, our journey to Dr. Llewellyn's surgery was mercifully brief.

Upon entering the surgery, we were greeted by a rather startling sight. From behind a screen at the far end of the room, a figure emerged, scalpel in hand, bending over a prone form. Hearing our entrance, the man straightened and turned to face us.

He was not the elderly, bespectacled physician I had anticipated, but a young man of striking physique, his bearing suggesting a man of good breeding. He was clad not in the traditional white coat of a surgeon, but in a black shirt and trousers, a leather apron stained with crimson protecting his attire. His white gloves, too, bore the telltale marks of his profession.

A moment later, a young woman, his assistant, I presumed, peered out from behind the screen. Her face, framed by a mass of dark curls, was strikingly beautiful, her expression a mixture of curiosity and annoyance at our intrusion. In stark contrast to Dr. Llewellyn's impassive countenance, her eyes flashed with a silent accusation.

"Even in the face of tragedy, gentlemen," Dr. Llewellyn remarked, his voice cool and detached, "a private practitioner cannot abandon his patients." I was uncertain whether his words were intended as a subtle rebuke to my own profession, or merely a statement of fact.

"Dr. John Watson, at your service," I replied, stepping forward. "Of Baker Street."

"Ah, a fellow physician," Dr. Llewellyn acknowledged with a curt nod. "Welcome. I was just attending to a minor surgical procedure."

"I am accompanied by my friend, Mr. Sherlock Holmes," I continued. "He is a private detective, and a consultant to Scotland Yard. We are here at the behest of Mr. Lusk, regarding the recent murder."

"If you would be so kind as to wait a moment, gentlemen," Dr. Llewellyn replied, disappearing once more behind the screen. "I am nearly finished. Please, take a seat."

We settled ourselves upon a pair of chairs, the rhythmic rasp of the doctor's instruments audible through the thin partition. The swift, precise movements suggested a skilled hand, one well-versed in the delicate art of surgery.

A moment later, Dr. Llewellyn emerged from behind the screen, his gloves and scalpel still bearing the crimson stains of his recent endeavors. "This was no ordinary murder, gentlemen," he stated, his voice devoid of emotion. "The precision of the wounds, the manner in which the body was... dissected, suggests a perpetrator with a particular set of skills." He paused, his gaze fixed upon the blood-stained instruments in his hand. "The stomach, for instance, was laid open with such expertise that the intestines protruded. I myself was obliged to replace them before the body was transported to the mortuary."

Holmes shot a look at Lusk, a silent reprimand for the doctor's interference with the crime scene.

"Such a feat could not have been accomplished with a common blade," Dr. Llewellyn continued, holding up the scalpel for our inspection. "The weapon employed was undoubtedly slender and sharp, much like this surgical instrument." He spoke with a hint of professional pride, the blood-stained blade glinting ominously in the morning light.

We exchanged uneasy glances, the implications of the doctor's words hanging heavy in the air.

7.

Dr. Llewellyn, with a swift, practiced movement, sliced the air with his scalpel, the gesture mimicking the fatal wound inflicted upon the victim. The chillingly familiar arc of the blade sent a shiver down my spine.

"However," he explained, setting the scalpel aside, "the weapon used would have required a sturdier handle, one capable of delivering the necessary force for such a brutal act. A scalpel, delicate as it is, would prove inadequate." He mimed a stabbing motion, his grip firm and forceful. "Something akin to a cobbler's knife, perhaps, or a cork cutter."

He placed the blood-stained scalpel upon a nearby tray, and his assistant, with a practiced efficiency, whisked it away, returning a moment later with a basin of water for the doctor to cleanse his hands.

Holmes, his brow furrowed in thought, seemed to be turning the doctor's words over in his mind, testing their validity against the evidence we had observed. As Dr. Llewellyn finished washing his hands, he glanced up at my companion, who nodded slowly, a sign of agreement.

The doctor, drying his hands with a proffered towel, settled into a chair opposite us, a weary sigh escaping his lips. He stretched out his legs, his posture suggesting a man who had presented his case and now awaited the verdict.

"The blade, however," Holmes remarked, his voice sharp and incisive, "could not have been excessively long. We observed that the tip had scraped against the victim's vertebrae, indicating a length shorter than the thickness of her neck."

Dr. Llewellyn nodded in agreement. "Indeed, Mr. Holmes, your reasoning is sound. I believe Dr. Watson would concur."

I affirmed my agreement with a nod, and Dr. Llewellyn inclined his head in acknowledgment.

"However," he continued, his voice taking on a more urgent tone, "the length of the blade is a secondary concern. The true mystery lies in the absence of blood. Where is it, Mr. Holmes? Where is the blood?"

Holmes, his gaze fixed upon the doctor's face, seemed to be peering into the very depths of his soul. Then, with the sudden, decisive movements I had come to associate with moments of inspiration, he rose from his chair and approached Dr. Llewellyn.

He leaned forward, his posture reminiscent of an actor about to make a dramatic entrance, silently requesting permission to proceed with a demonstration. Lusk, with a courteous nod, granted his assent.

Holmes placed the fingers of his right hand firmly over Dr. Llewellyn's mouth. The doctor, understanding the purpose of this unexpected gesture, remained impassive.

"The killer, I believe, would have silenced his victim in this manner," Holmes explained, his voice low and intense. "The nature of the wound suggests the throat was cut while the unfortunate woman's cries were stifled. This explains the lack of witnesses, the absence of any reported disturbance." He withdrew his hand, his left fist clenching as if gripping a phantom blade. With a swift, chilling motion, he mimed a slashing movement across Dr. Llewellyn's throat.

"The act itself would have been swift, brutal, leaving the victim little time to comprehend her fate."

He paused, his gaze fixed upon the imaginary blood now staining his hand. "The killer, in this scenario, would be drenched in his victim's blood. He would see her terror, her pain, and in that moment, his own bloodlust would be satiated."

"This explains," he concluded, "why there was so little blood upon the body itself. The majority would have been transferred to the perpetrator."

"But how could a man, so covered in blood, escape unnoticed?" Lusk inquired, his brow furrowed in perplexity.

"He would have been wearing an apron, much like this one," Holmes replied, gesturing towards the blood-stained garment still adorning Dr. Llewellyn.

The doctor, no fool, understood the implication.

Was it possible, I wondered, that the physician before us was the very killer we sought? I glanced at Holmes, who was now scrutinizing the doctor's apron with an intensity that bordered on suspicion.

"Such aprons are not ubiquitous, Mr. Holmes," Dr. Llewellyn countered, rising to his feet and removing the blood-stained garment, which he had, until now, forgotten to discard. "They are the tools of our trade, worn by those of us who deal in blood, both in its giving and its taking."

"Are you suggesting, then," Holmes inquired, his gaze lingering upon the crimson stains, "that a fellow physician is responsible for this atrocity?"

"One need not possess a medical degree to wield a blade with such precision," Dr. Llewellyn replied, his tone clipped. "A butcher, for instance, could be equally adept at such a task." It was clear that he resented the implication, the suggestion that one of his own profession could be capable of such barbarity.

Before Holmes could press the matter further, a groan emanated from behind the screen, a reminder of the doctor's other patient.

Dr. Llewellyn, with a muttered apology, hastily handed his apron to his assistant, who had materialized silently at his side. She took the garment without a word, disappearing once more behind the screen.

"My apologies, gentlemen," Dr. Llewellyn said, his voice now carrying a hint of urgency. "It seems I neglected to administer a pain reliever to my patient." His words, though addressed to us, were clearly intended for his assistant's ears as well.

With a shake of his head, he indicated that our interview was at an end. We rose from our chairs, a sense of unease lingering in the air.

Holmes, I noticed, pinched his lower lip, a habit he often displayed when suppressing a surge of questions. We departed the surgery, each of us lost in our own thoughts.

8.

Lusk, ever the gracious host, insisted we join him for luncheon at his residence. Following a repast that did much to restore our spirits, we made our way, at a more leisurely pace, back to the mortuary.

Upon entering the somber building, we found a group of five or six women awaiting our arrival. The mortuary attendant, having already taken their statements, kindly provided us with a summary of their accounts.

"This lady," he said, gesturing towards a woman of dignified bearing, "is the matron of the Lambeth Girls' House, whom we escorted here at your request, Mr. Holmes."

"And yet," he continued, his tone laced with a hint of accusation, "she claims to be unable to identify the deceased."

"What of the markings upon her undergarments?" Holmes inquired, his voice sharp and alert.

"The markings are indeed consistent with those used by our institution," the matron conceded, "but they could have been issued some years ago. I cannot be certain."

"Very well, madam," Holmes replied. "You are free to go."

The matron, visibly relieved, departed with a hasty curtsy.

Holmes turned his attention to the remaining women. "These ladies," the attendant explained, "were brought here by our constables who visited the public houses in the area. Word of the murder had spread, and they came forward, hoping to ascertain whether the victim was one of their acquaintance. They believe a woman resembling the deceased resided in a public house on Thrawl Street, in Spitalfields."

"And did you allow them to view the body?" Holmes inquired.

"Indeed, sir," the attendant replied. "I dismissed those who could not make an identification. These three, however, recognized the woman as their friend, Polly."

"Not a friend, sir," one of the women interjected, her voice sharp and defensive. She was a slender woman, her attire suggesting a life lived on the fringes of society, much like the deceased. "Polly was merely a lodger, sharing a room with us three at the public house on Thrawl Street." Her companions nodded in agreement, their faces grim. It was clear she had become the spokesperson for the trio.

"We rented the room together," she explained, "each contributing to the rent as our means allowed. We had separate beds, of course."

Holmes leaned towards Lusk, his voice a low murmur. "It appears my initial assessment was correct. This unfortunate woman was, as I suspected, one of the 'unfortunates'." He then settled into a chair facing the three women, his gaze intent, inviting them to share their knowledge.

The two of us took our seats by his side.

"Tell me," Holmes began, his voice laced with a keen interest, "what can you tell me about Polly?"

"We knew little of her personal life, sir," the woman replied, her gaze fixed upon her lap. "She had been lodging with us for perhaps three weeks."

The other two women, though silent, seemed to be holding back information.

"Please," Holmes urged, his eyes meeting theirs directly, "tell me everything you know. Every detail, however insignificant it may seem, could prove vital to our investigation."

Under Holmes's penetrating gaze, the woman had little choice but to respond. She hesitated for a moment, as if mesmerized by his presence, then spoke in a hushed voice. "Thursday night, sir, Polly returned to the lodging house, but the landlord turned her out, for she had no money for the rent."

Her words seemed to loosen the tongues of her companions, and they began to chatter excitedly, their voices overlapping.

"She was drunk, sir," the second woman chimed in.

"Blind drunk," the third added.

"Indeed," the second continued, "when the landlord threw her out, she just laughed, a wild, strange laugh it was. 'I'll find the money soon enough,' she said, pointing to a gaudy hat adorned with flowers. 'Just look at this lovely hat!' Then she turned and walked away."

"I'd never seen her wear such a hat before," the first woman remarked, a puzzled frown creasing her brow.

"Aye, and off she went," the second concluded, their voices now a drunken chorus of agreement.

"And who is this lady?" Lusk inquired, gesturing towards a fourth woman who stood apart from the trio, her demeanor more composed.

Before the attendant could reply, the woman spoke. "I'm a neighbour, sir. I heard these ladies were coming here to see if the poor soul was Polly, so I thought I'd come along. I saw her myself, after she was turned out of the lodging house, around half past two Friday morning."

"Where was this?" Holmes asked, his interest piqued.

"On Whitechapel Road, sir," the woman replied. "Just across from the church, where it meets Osborne Street."

Lusk, I noticed, gripped his cane tightly, his gaze darting between Holmes and the woman. "That's less than five hundred yards from where the body was found," he murmured, his voice tight with concern.

"Monk knows Polly well, don't she?" one of the other women interjected, a sudden recollection dawning upon her. Her companions nodded in agreement.

The women, having given their accounts, departed, promising to send the woman called Monk to the mortuary as soon as possible.

We settled in for a long wait, the atmosphere thick with anticipation. Holmes, ever restless, retreated to the inner sanctum of the mortuary, seeking further clues amongst the grim evidence. Lusk and I, left to our own devices, attempted to distract ourselves with the evening papers.

True to their word, the women sent Mary Anne Monk to the mortuary shortly after half past six. She confirmed that the deceased, known to her as Polly from their shared time at a public house, was in fact Mary Anne Nichols. Monk herself was employed at the Lambeth House for Girls, a workhouse where she and Nichols had been colleagues the previous year. She had been deeply saddened by the news of the murder, and had waited anxiously for her shift to end before coming to the mortuary.

According to Monk, Nichols had left the workhouse in May, taking a position as a housemaid in Wandsworth. However, she had been dismissed after being caught stealing three pounds from her employers. Monk had encountered her friend some six weeks prior, and Nichols had confided in her about her misfortune.

After examining the body carefully, Monk confirmed, with a heavy heart, that it was indeed her friend, Polly Nichols. She explained that they were both named Mary Anne, but to avoid confusion, she was known as Monk, while her friend went by Polly.

Lusk, ever generous, pressed a handsome sum into Holmes's hand, and with a gracious nod of farewell, hailed a carriage to convey us back to Baker Street.

9.

Thanks to Holmes's keen deductions, the identity of the unfortunate Polly, or Mary Anne Nichols as she was formally known, was swiftly established. However, the identity of her murderer, and the motive behind the brutal slaying, remained a mystery.

Holmes, I knew, had not abandoned the case. He spent the following week ensconced upon the sofa, enveloped in a haze of pipe smoke, his mind grappling with the complexities of the crime. A shadow of preoccupation lingered upon his features, a sign that some aspect of the case troubled him deeply. I, however, forbore from questioning him, knowing that he would confide in me when he deemed it appropriate.

The sitting room was littered with newspapers, each bearing lurid accounts of the Whitechapel murder. "Thousands of Prostitutes in London – A Shame to Our Nation!" screamed one headline, a testament to the sensationalist nature of the press. It seemed that scandal and gossip sold more papers than factual reporting. Scotland Yard, I noted, had assigned Detective Inspector Frederick Abberline to the case, a man renowned for his tenacity and investigative prowess.

"How do these reporters come by such detailed information so quickly?" I inquired, my curiosity piqued by the sheer volume of speculation and conjecture that filled the pages.

"It is an open secret, Watson," Holmes replied, his voice calm and measured, "that certain members of the constabulary supplement their incomes by providing the press with, shall we say, 'advance intelligence' on ongoing investigations." He pointed to a headline on a discarded newspaper. "They've assigned Abberline to the case. A shrewd move, for he is undoubtedly one of Scotland Yard's finest."

"Indeed," I agreed, "though I confess I find it curious that a man of Abberline's stature would be tasked with investigating the murder of a common prostitute. Similarly, why would a man of Lusk's standing – a gentleman, a Freemason – entrust such a matter to us? It seems rather... incongruous."

Holmes's gaze met mine, a flicker of unease in his eyes. "I suspect, Watson, that there are forces at play here that we do not fully comprehend. They are attempting to manipulate us, to steer our inquiries in a particular direction. It is as if the very fabric of East London is unraveling, and those in power are desperate to maintain control."

He gestured towards the scattered newspapers, his gaze sweeping over the lurid headlines as if searching for a hidden message. "Did you note the haste with which the authorities sought to conceal the details of the crime? The body removed with indecent speed, the scene scrubbed clean, the post-mortem conducted with an almost frantic urgency, leaving Abberline with precious little to work with."

"Why go to such lengths to cover up the murder of a mere prostitute?" I asked, perplexed.

"Precisely, Watson," Holmes replied, his voice taking on a sharper edge. "If the murder of this woman is deemed so significant, it stands to reason that the killer himself must be a person of consequence." He paused, his eyes narrowing in thought. "I have it on good authority that even Mr. Lees, the Queen's own astrologer, has been consulted in this matter."

Holmes rose from the sofa and settled into his armchair by the fire, leaving the newspapers scattered upon the floor. I remained silent, allowing him to pursue his train of thought undisturbed. His gaze, though fixed upon the flickering flames, seemed to be focused inward, upon some unseen puzzle.

"It strikes me as curious, Watson," he remarked at length, "that none of the residents on the opposite side of Bucks Row reported hearing any disturbance. Eight families reside there, yet not a single soul witnessed or heard anything untoward."

"Perhaps it is the nature of Whitechapel, Holmes," I suggested. "A place where people turn a blind eye to the darkness that surrounds them. A place where it is safer to see no evil, hear no evil."

Holmes turned to me, his gaze intense, and his voice low and urgent. "This is no ordinary murder, Watson. There is something amiss, something that does not ring true. The lack of blood at the scene, the very fact that the body was moved so hastily... it all points to a deliberate attempt to conceal the true nature of the crime." He paused, his brow furrowed in thought. "Furthermore, I have been examining the witness statements, and I find a curious discrepancy in Dr. Llewellyn's initial account. He makes no mention of the abdominal wounds, stating only that the victim's throat had been cut and that he had pronounced her dead."

"But surely..." I began, my mind reeling from this revelation. Even without Holmes voicing his suspicions, I could sense that Dr. Llewellyn had become a person of interest in this macabre affair.

Before Holmes could elaborate, a sharp rapping at the door interrupted our conversation. A messenger, his face flushed with urgency, stood upon the threshold, a telegram clutched in his hand.

"Urgent, sir!" he exclaimed, thrusting the missive towards Holmes.

Holmes unfolded the telegram, his eyes scanning the brief message.

'Another one! Come to Hanbury Street' - Lusk.

10.

We made haste to ready ourselves and procured a carriage to Hanbury Street. As we traversed the labyrinthine thoroughfares, approaching Spitalfield, a palpable gloom descended upon the vicinity, as though the very air itself recoiled from the heinous act perpetrated within its midst. Alighting from our conveyance near the rear of Number 29, Hanbury Street, it became immediately apparent that the unfortunate soul had not been removed from the scene. A throng had congregated – constables, gawkers, and the esteemed gentleman Lusk amongst them.

A shiver coursed down my spine. Was the killer who wrought this carnage present amongst us? Were his eyes, even now, scanning for his next victim? Would my own fate be intertwined with his macabre design? A dread, cold and formidable, seized me. Perspiration beaded upon my brow, and a wave of nausea washed over me. My gaze darted from face to face, searching for any telltale sign, any flicker of madness that might betray the killer's presence. And then, I saw it.

Whether the constables were taking statements or attempting to disperse the crowd, I could not discern. But as I stepped from the carriage, my eyes, looking beyond the gathered crowd, beheld the full spectacle of the scene beyond. The sight struck me with the force of a physical blow, shaking me to my very core.

Vertigo threatened to consume me, and for a fleeting moment, I felt as though life itself were draining from my body. I, who had borne witness to the horrors of the Afghan campaign, who had, by virtue of my profession, become inured to the sight of blood and suffering, I, who had endured the agony of my own mangled limb, was yet utterly undone by the ghastly tableau before me. Hyperbole, I assure you, has no place in this account; never before had I encountered such unmitigated savagery.

As my vision cleared and the murmuring of the crowd resolved itself into coherent speech, the first words to penetrate my consciousness were those of Lusk, striding towards us, his face grim. "No need to wonder where the blood is this time, gentlemen," he remarked, devoid of mirth.

It was only then, as I fought to regain mastery over my senses, that I noticed Holmes, his usually stoic countenance etched with a profound astonishment, his gaze fixed upon the gruesome spectacle before us.

11.

We arrived at the macabre scene a quarter before the hour of seven. The ill-fated woman had been discovered in the bleak light of dawn, lying lifeless in a desolate lane adjacent to a tenement yard on Hanbury Street. Her throat, like that of the unfortunate Miss Nichols, had been savagely severed.

"Scarcely a half-mile separates this gruesome discovery from the site of Nichols' demise," Holmes murmured, his voice low and grave, his gaze fixed upon the appalling spectacle before us.

"The task of identifying the deceased has, mercifully, already been seen to," Lusk informed us, his tone betraying the strain of the investigation. "The name of the unfortunate soul is Annie

Chapman. Like Miss Nichols, she walked among the shadows of life, a member of what some might term the 'unfortunate class'."

An officer approached, his face drawn. "A woman, professing to be acquainted with the victim, has stated that Miss Chapman departed in the dead of night, seeking, it seems, a patron to alleviate her financial burdens."

It was evident that Lusk had apprised his men of Holmes' involvement, instructing them to afford him their full cooperation. Yet, our attention remained inexorably drawn to the mutilated form that lay sprawled upon the cobblestones. Her throat, as previously noted, had been cruelly slit; her abdomen, however, bore the mark of even greater savagery, ripped asunder with a ferocity that defied comprehension. Her entrails lay scattered upon the ground, a testament to the depravity of her assailant.

"The perpetrator," Holmes declared, his voice sharp with deduction, "lingered here for a considerable duration after the deed was done. Such barbarity cannot be wrought in haste." He paused, his gaze sweeping over the scene. "He sought not merely to extinguish life, Watson, but to utterly despoil it. Observe." He gestured towards an object lying near the body.

I followed his indication, my stomach churning with a sickening dread. Alas, my medical training left me in no doubt as to the nature of the gruesome relic. My head swam, and I fought back the urge to retch. The heart and liver, removed with chilling precision, had been placed upon the cobblestones, a grotesque offering beside the mutilated corpse.

Averting my gaze from this ghastly detail, I attempted to take in the entirety of the scene. The victim, Annie Chapman, I estimated to be of slight stature, perhaps five feet two or three inches in height. Her hair, matted with blood, was a dark auburn, curling slightly at the edges. Her eyes, wide with the terror of her final moments, were a startling blue, staring vacantly upwards.

Her face, contorted in a silent scream of terror, spoke volumes of the sudden and unexpected nature of her demise. Her nose was broad, and I observed, with a chilling sense of déjà vu, that she bore a striking resemblance to the hapless Mary Anne Nichols, her front teeth similarly marred by the loss of two incisors. She was clad, though simply, in a respectable manner, her form covered by two worn coats, though notably lacking any headwear. Beneath lay a plain skirt and blouse.

With a practiced eye, Holmes drew near the body, his movements deft, avoiding the pools of blood and scattered viscera. He carefully examined the contents of her pockets, extracting a lone item of interest – an envelope bearing the insignia of the Sussex Regiment. Holmes retreated from the immediate vicinity of the corpse, his path measured and precise, like a man navigating stepping stones across a treacherous mire.

"At a quarter past the hour of six," Lusk began, his voice heavy with the weight of his responsibilities, "the spectre of fear once again descended upon Whitechapel. News of this latest atrocity reached me with utmost haste, and I wasted no time in attending the scene. Another unfortunate soul, slain with a brutality that chills the very marrow. I immediately dispatched a telegram to summon your unique talents, Mr. Holmes." He paused, his gaze sweeping over the assembled constables and gawkers. "We stand now in Hanbury Street, formerly known as Brown Street, in the heart of Spitalfield. Our victim, as you have no doubt ascertained, is one Annie Chapman, a woman of twenty-nine years. You will have observed, in your journey here, that Hanbury Street lies nestled between Commercial Street and Whitechapel Road. The inhabitants of this thoroughfare, however, bear little resemblance to their more affluent neighbours. Poverty casts a long shadow here, Mr. Holmes, and the majority of residents are immigrant Jews."

"The parallels to the Bucks Row affair are undeniable," Holmes remarked, drawing a deep, weary breath. I was struck by this uncharacteristic display of emotion; never before had I witnessed such a visible sign of empathy from the man who often seemed more akin to a calculating machine than a creature of flesh and blood. "The modus operandi, the proximity of the two murders... it does not bode well."

Leaning closer, he murmured in my ear, his voice barely a whisper, "It appears we are faced with a killer of singular depravity, Watson. A serial killer, to employ the modern parlance."

At that moment, Lusk approached, accompanied by a tall, officious-looking constable. "Gentlemen," Lusk announced, "allow me to introduce Officer Longmore, the officer charged with overseeing this investigation. He has graciously consented to share the fruits of his inquiries with Mr. Holmes and to offer his full cooperation in our endeavours."

Officer Longmore, dispensing with any pleasantries, launched directly into his report, his hand gesturing towards the lifeless form of Annie Chapman. "The deceased," he stated, his voice devoid of inflection, "was known to frequent this neighbourhood, a member of the so-called 'unfortunate' class, much like our previous victim. She answered, it seems, to the rather colourful sobriquet of 'Annie Sivvy', though her true name, we have ascertained, is indeed Annie Chapman. Those acquainted with the woman speak of her with a surprising degree of respect, despite her unfortunate circumstances."

I confess, the question of what constituted "respectability" in the context of these unfortunate women lingered in my mind. However, the inherent delicacy of the subject, coupled with the evident sensitivity of those present, dissuaded me from giving voice to my query.

Officer Longmore, continuing his report, gestured towards the dwelling adjacent to the scene. "The murder," he elaborated, "transpired in close proximity to the rear of the residence belonging to a Mrs. Richardson. The woman operates a modest enterprise in her basement, employing several hands in the production of cat food."

True to form, Holmes commenced his meticulous examination of the crime scene, his keen eyes scanning the mutilated body and its surroundings. I, meanwhile, accompanied Lusk on a circuit of the garden, hoping against hope that some vital clue might present itself to our scrutiny.

A narrow passage, terminating in a door, provided access from the upper level of the house to a small porch, perhaps thirteen or fourteen feet in length. A wooden fence separated this meagre outdoor space from the neighbouring property. I noted with interest that the porch offered no secondary exit; entry and egress were seemingly limited to this single point.

The garden itself was cluttered with stacks of freshly delivered packaging materials, leaving only a narrow path from the back door to a small clearing at the far end. It was in this secluded corner, shielded from casual observation, that the murder had evidently taken place.

Officer Longmore, I gathered, was firm in his conviction that the unfortunate deed had occurred within the confines of the house, the body subsequently dragged out to the garden. In support of this theory, he pointed to a trail of blood leading from the back door to the spot where the victim now lay.

Holmes, however, remained unconvinced. "The very location of the murder," he countered, "argues against the inspector's hypothesis. This corner of the garden lies directly within the blind spot of the door. Even were it standing open, one could not readily perceive events unfolding at such a distance. The killer, we must assume, was intimately familiar with this layout."

The trail of blood, he explained, was easily explained. The packaging materials, stacked as they were near the site of the murder, had been hastily moved indoors, presumably to protect them from the elements once the discovery of the body attracted a crowd. The blood, seeping into the edges of the boxes, had thus been inadvertently tracked towards the house. This theory was swiftly corroborated; the boxes were indeed found inside, and the workers readily admitted to having moved them prior to the arrival of the constabulary. Mrs. Richardson, the owner of the property, confirmed that she had instructed her employees to do so.

With the initial examination of the crime scene complete, and Holmes offering no objection, Officer Longmore directed that the body be conveyed to the mortuary on Eagle Street. A Spitalfields ambulance, its arrival lending a further air of grim reality to the proceedings, bore the lifeless form of Annie Chapman away.

Our inquiries now turned to the collation and analysis of witness statements, a task as vital as it was often tedious. The evidence thus far gathered pointed towards a timeframe for the murder shortly before half past five in the morning.

A statement from one Albert Cadosch, a resident of the adjacent property, proved particularly intriguing. Cadosch, it transpired, had risen early that morning, venturing out to the outhouse situated beside his dwelling, at approximately twenty-five minutes past five. It was during this time, he reported, that his ears were drawn to a muffled exchange emanating from beyond the garden wall.

"I distinctly heard a voice cry out, 'Don't!'," Cadosch recounted, his brow furrowed in recollection. "The words that followed were indistinct. Then, silence."

"And yet you took no further action?" Officer Longmore interjected, his tone sharp with incredulity.

"I saw no cause for alarm, sir," Cadosch protested. "I assumed it to be merely my neighbour, attending to his packaging materials in the garden. I gave it no further thought." He paused, adding somewhat sheepishly, "I was already behind schedule for work."

Further attempts to elicit additional details from the man proved fruitless.

"This location warrants closer scrutiny," Holmes declared, his gaze sweeping over the cramped confines of the garden. "And Mr.

Longmore, we must question each and every resident of this house. A laborious undertaking, to be sure, but essential nonetheless."

Longmore, nodding his assent, departed in the company of a fellow constable to commence the arduous task of interviewing the occupants of the house.

Despite the compact nature of the yard, the dwelling itself, it transpired, housed no fewer than six families. The inhabitants of the ground floor, roused from their slumber, could offer no insight into the events of the previous night or that morning, claiming to have neither seen nor heard anything untoward.

"It seems evident," Holmes remarked, his eyes narrowed in thought, "that the door leading from the front of the house to the rear yard is customarily left unlocked for the convenience of the residents." This deduction was met with nods of confirmation from the assembled tenants.

One by one, the inhabitants of the house were summoned for questioning. The first to be brought before us was a man by the name of John Davies, the individual who had stumbled upon the grisly scene that morning. Davies, a porter by trade at the bustling Spitalfield Market, cut a nervous figure, clutching a grimy cap in his hands and scratching his head repeatedly.

"When I first clapped eyes on the body, sir," he stammered, "I dared not even approach to ascertain whether the poor woman yet lived. Fear, pure and consuming, seized me. I rushed back inside, alerting the other residents. It was they who confirmed her passing. I then made haste to the constabulary station on Commercial Street to report the matter."

The landlady, a Mrs. Richardson, was next to be interviewed. She had occupied a room on the second floor, accompanied by a young woman named Elisa Cukelly. Both had been roused from their slumber by the commotion emanating from the lower level of the house.

"I feared the dwelling was ablaze," Mrs. Richardson declared, her voice trembling slightly. "The noise was most alarming. I hastened to the window, and it was then that I beheld the unfortunate creature, sprawled upon the cobblestones, her skirts obscenely disarrayed. I rushed downstairs and saw with my own eyes the dreadful mutilation that had been inflicted upon her. I instructed one of the lads employed in my service to see to the poor woman's modesty, assuring him that I would bear any responsibility for the act. Even in death, I reasoned, a woman deserves a measure of dignity." She paused, her gaze hardening. "I informed the constables of my actions upon their arrival, and they seemed to appreciate the sentiment, however unconventional."

Holmes shot me a curious glance, his expression unreadable. Uncertain whether to align myself with his apparent skepticism or the constabulary's acceptance of the landlady's account, I turned to Detective Longmore. He offered a curt nod, confirming the veracity of Mrs. Richardson's statement.

"The woman speaks the truth, however unpleasant," Longmore conceded. "The savagery visited upon the victim was truly horrific."

He let the statement hang in the air, the unspoken details lingering like a miasma. I glanced back at Holmes, who now, too, nodded his agreement, his face grave.

"The nature and position of the wounds," Holmes observed, his voice betraying a hint of grim satisfaction, "coupled with the distribution of bloodstains upon the garden wall, strongly suggest that the fatal blow was struck while the victim lay supine."

12.

We had initially deemed it unnecessary to attend the post-mortem examination of the unfortunate Miss Chapman. The gruesome display at the crime scene, her internal organs laid bare for all to see, had led us to the premature conclusion that the pathologist's scalpel would reveal little more of consequence.

How profoundly mistaken we were.

News reached us, swift and chilling, that the victim's womb was missing. This crucial detail, inexplicably overlooked amidst the carnage in the garden, sent us hurrying to the mortuary on Eagle Street with the utmost haste.

Upon arriving at the somber edifice, we learned that the post-mortem examination had yielded a grim parallel to the murder of Mary Anne Nichols. The Whitechapel killer, it seemed, harboured a macabre fascination with a particular trophy; the womb, absent from both victims, bore silent witness to his depravity.

The mortuary hall, accessed via a set of imposing green double doors, was a scene of subdued activity. A contingent of constables stood in a loose circle around the shrouded form of Annie Chapman, their faces etched with a mixture of disgust and morbid curiosity.

Dr. Phillips, the pathologist charged with the unenviable task of examining the remains, approached us, his countenance betraying the strain of the morning's work. "Gentlemen," he greeted us, his voice weary, and "a most unfortunate development. We initially rearranged the displaced organs, restoring them to their natural positions within the body cavity, before commencing a standard examination. It was only then that the missing organ became apparent."

"The incisions," Dr. Phillips announced, his gaze sweeping over the assembled company – Lusk, Detective Abberline, Holmes, and myself – "bear the unmistakable hallmarks of the weapon employed in the previous murder."

He paused, letting the gravity of his pronouncement sink in, before delivering his chilling summation: "Same cut, same knife, and same killer." The words hung in the air, heavy with implication, silencing the unspoken questions that lingered in our minds.

Holmes, ever eager to apply his formidable intellect to the puzzle before us, stepped forward to examine the body. Detective Abberline and his subordinate, their faces tight with disapproval, exchanged a curt nod with Lusk before exiting the room. Dr. Phillips later confided in me that a heated exchange had transpired between Lusk and Abberline regarding the wisdom of involving a private detective in the investigation, a move that Abberline clearly perceived as an indictment of the constabulary's competence. It dawned on me then that this simmering tension within the ranks of Scotland Yard was, in no small part, responsible for our presence in that stark chamber of death.

Having completed his examination, Holmes straightened, his expression thoughtful. "While the deceased appears to have been reasonably well-nourished," he observed, gesturing towards the body, "certain areas – the breasts, the knees, the elbows – exhibit a degree of wear and tear inconsistent with her otherwise healthy constitution." He paused, his gaze lingering on the lifeless form. "These are telltale signs of a life lived in the shadows, a profession, shall we say, not known for its gentle touch."

Dr. Phillips, momentarily distracted from his ongoing debate with a colleague regarding the precise sequence of fatal wounds, shot Holmes a look of mingled surprise and disapproval. He then proceeded to shroud the body once more, issuing strict instructions to the attending constables that it was to remain undisturbed until further notice. I could not help but surmise that the pathologist's haste to cover the remains stemmed, at least in part, from a sense of propriety offended by my friend's blunt assessment of the victim's profession.

Leaning closer to Lusk, who sat hunched in contemplation nearby, I murmured, "I must confess, I am somewhat surprised by my friend's discretion in this matter. He is not typically one to mince words, yet he chose to merely allude to the woman's line of work rather than pronounce it outright."

"Indeed," Lusk replied, a wry smile flickering across his lips. "It appears even Sherlock Holmes is capable of exercising a modicum of tact when the occasion demands it."

13.

That evening, the District Coroner, a man of stern countenance and imposing presence, arrived at the mortuary. With a wave of his hand, he dismissed the younger constables from the premises, citing the sensitive nature of the pathologist's findings. He then turned his attention to the assembled members of the press, his gaze sharp and unforgiving. "Gentlemen," he admonished, "I trust you will exercise the utmost discretion in your reporting of this case. Sensationalism has no place in matters such as these."

Dr. Phillips, thus prompted, stepped forward to deliver his findings. "The victim's entrails," he began, his voice devoid of emotion, "had been entirely severed from their mesenteric attachments and placed upon her shoulders. The angle of the incisions, I must emphasize, is of particular interest." He paused, drawing a finger across his own throat in a chillingly illustrative gesture. "The cuts run consistently from left to right, indicating that the perpetrator wielded the murder weapon in his left hand, rather than his right."

He continued, his words painting a gruesome picture for those assembled. "Furthermore, the womb, along with its associated ligaments, as well as a significant portion of the urinary bladder – approximately two-thirds, I would estimate – had been excised. The upper portion of the vagina was similarly removed."

"Tell me, Doctor," the Coroner inquired, his brow furrowed in thought, "were these organs removed individually, or en masse?"

"Individually, sir," Dr. Phillips confirmed.

"Might we then deduce the involvement of someone with medical training?"

"I think not," the pathologist replied, shaking his head. "No trained physician would inflict such wanton destruction upon a human body."

"Are you suggesting, then, that the perpetrator is a madman?"

"On the contrary, sir," Dr. Phillips countered. "The precision of the excisions speaks to a chilling level of calculation. These organs were removed with deliberate intent, one by one. A skilled surgeon, I might add, would require no less than fifteen minutes to accomplish such a feat."

"Thank you, Doctor," the Coroner acknowledged, rising from his seat. "Your insights prove most illuminating. We shall require your further testimony on the morrow." He then addressed the room at large, announcing, "A formal inquest shall convene tomorrow, Monday, at half past ten, at my offices near Whitechapel Railway station. All witnesses are expected to attend."

With that, the proceedings drew to a close. We filed out of the mortuary, our thoughts a maelstrom of speculation and unease. Detective Abberline, his face a mask of grim determination, stood engaged in hushed conversation with Dr. Phillips near the entrance. We nodded our farewells and made our way past them, stepping out into the cool night air.

"The killer, it seems, was in no hurry to complete his gruesome task," Holmes remarked, his voice low and thoughtful, as we hailed a passing hansom. "He took his time, savouring the act, if such a word can be uttered in connection with such barbarity."

We climbed into the waiting carriage and as the hansom rattled towards Baker Street, I could not shake the feeling that we had only just glimpsed the depths of the darkness that had descended upon Whitechapel.

14.

The morning edition of The London Times lay upon our doorstep, deposited there with a customary thud by the punctual paperboy. I retrieved the broadsheet, only to be met by a headline that sent a jolt through me: "Another Gruesome Murder!" For a fleeting moment, I entertained the absurd notion that a fresh atrocity had occurred during the night, so closely did the words mirror my own recent experience.

A glance at the date, however, confirmed that the paper dealt with the horrors we had witnessed the previous day. The account, I noted with a mixture of fascination and revulsion, was remarkably detailed, as though the journalist himself had stood witness to the carnage.

Peering out of our window, I observed that copies of The Times were being snapped up with an almost feverish intensity. Passersby, their faces etched with a mixture of horror and morbid curiosity, paused to exchange pennies for the latest news. It was as though the entire city had fallen under a spell, united in their morbid fascination with the unfolding drama in Whitechapel.

Holmes, seemingly unperturbed by the palpable tension that had gripped the city, calmly proceeded to fill his pipe.

I settled into my armchair and began to peruse the account. The journalist, I was forced to concede, had painted a vivid, if somewhat sensationalized, picture of the scene on Hanbury Street. "East London's Terror!" screamed one subheading. "Victim Cut to Pieces!" declared another. "Whitechapel in Chaos!" Each headline seemed more outlandish than the last, designed to inflame the reader's imagination and send shivers down their spine.

Even I, who had witnessed the aftermath of the murder firsthand, found myself strangely affected by the lurid prose. The physician in me recognized the telltale signs of heightened blood pressure, the quickening pulse, the clammy grip of fear.

Holmes, sensing my agitation, reached across and gently extracted the paper from my grasp. Pipe in one hand, he scanned the page with an intensity that belied his earlier indifference. "Another Gruesome Murder!" he read aloud, his voice tinged with a hint of amusement. He seemed to regard the death of a fellow human being as nothing more than an intriguing puzzle, a welcome opportunity to exercise his considerable intellect.

"This latest development complicates matters considerably!" I exclaimed, but my words were met with silence. Holmes, lost in the labyrinthine world of the case, seemed oblivious to my presence.

"I must confess," I continued, emboldened by his silence, "that even having seen the dreadful sight with my own eyes, the headline momentarily led me to believe that another murder had transpired."

Holmes finally lowered the paper, fixing me with a gaze that bordered on bemusement. "My dear Watson," he said, setting aside his pipe and pouring me a glass of water from the decanter on the mantlepiece, "such a reaction is entirely understandable, if somewhat illogical." He relit his pipe, settling back into his chair with an air of languid contentment. "This latest turn of events, while undoubtedly tragic, merely provides us with additional data points, further clues to aid us in our pursuit of the truth."

"But at what cost?" I retorted, unable to contain my frustration. "Must we sacrifice yet another life upon the altar of your deductions? Can we not strive to prevent these atrocities, rather than merely seeking to solve them after the fact?"

Holmes, his brow furrowed in thought, regarded me with an intensity that suggested he was reading far more than my words alone conveyed. For a long moment, he remained silent.

We arrived at the Coroner's inquest just as the clock chimed the appointed hour. The room was filled to capacity, a throng of journalists, curious onlookers, and stern-faced constables vying for space within its walls. I spotted Lusk and Detective Abberline occupying seats in the front row, their faces drawn and weary. Dr. Phillips, the pathologist, sat hunched in his chair.

Holmes and I, choosing to remain inconspicuous, settled into seats at the back of the room, our senses alert to the murmur of speculation that rippled through the assembled company. Lusk and Abberline, I observed, were engaged in a heated, though whispered, exchange, and their disagreement evident even from our distant vantage point. The arrival of the Coroner, however, brought their conversation to an abrupt halt.

A hush fell over the room as the Coroner, his face a mask of professional detachment, took his place at the head of the table. The inquest, he announced, would proceed in an orderly fashion, with each witness called upon to provide their account of the events surrounding the untimely demise of Miss Annie Chapman.

A succession of witnesses were called forth – constables, neighbours, casual passersby – their testimonies adding fragments of information to the emerging, though still incomplete, picture of the crime. It was the statement of Mrs. Richardson, however, that proved most illuminating.

"I have resided at Number 29 Hanbury Street these past fifteen years," the landlady began, her voice firm despite the gravity of the occasion. "My tenants, while of modest means, are hardworking and honest folk. Some have rented rooms from me for upwards of twelve years." She paused, her gaze sweeping over the assembled company. "The majority find employment at the Billingsgate Fish Market or the Spitalfields Market. Their work often necessitates their departure at odd hours – one o'clock, four o'clock, even five o'clock in the morning. Consequently, the house is rarely locked. It stands open throughout the night, accessible to anyone who might care to enter."

She drew a deep breath, her expression hardening. "I believe that the deceased entered the garden of her own volition. Had there been a struggle, or a fight, surely someone would have heard. Several of my tenants occupy rooms adjacent to the porch, and it is not uncommon for windows to be left ajar during the warmer months. Yet, no one reports hearing anything untoward."

"One of my tenants, a Mr. Thompson, employed by the Godsons' over on Brick Lane, departed for work at four o'clock that morning. While he did not pass directly through the porch, he saw nothing amiss as he exited the house."

"My son, John, left for his own employment at ten minutes past five. He, too, saw nothing out of the ordinary."

"It was shortly before six o'clock when Mr. Davies, another of my tenants, made the gruesome discovery. He was descending the stairs when he spotted the woman's body lying in the corner of the garden, near the entrance to the house."

15.

Holmes and I hailed a passing hansom, our minds still awhirl with the details of the inquest, and settled back into the familiar discomfort of its worn leather seats. The journey back to Baker Street was a somber affair.

I found myself utterly drained, my stomach churning with a mixture of revulsion and a strange, unwelcome fascination with the gruesome details of the case. Holmes, as was his wont, retreated into the labyrinthine corridors of his mind, his face pale and drawn, his gaze fixed upon some distant point visible only to him.

The hansom rattled on, bearing us away from Whitechapel towards the relative tranquility of our Baker Street lodgings. The journey, usually a brisk half-hour affair to cover the five miles, seemed to stretch on interminably.

I longed to break the silence, however momentarily, from the grim images that danced before my mind's eye. Yet, the words seemed to catch in my throat, stifled by a strange mixture of exhaustion and a growing sense of dread.

As our hansom clattered past the bustling thoroughfare of Commercial Street, leaving the grim confines of Whitechapel behind us, and turned onto Old Street, having traversed the length of Great Eastern Street, Holmes stirred from his reverie.

"There is a matter, Watson," he began, his voice low and serious, "that I feel compelled to address."

The silence we had maintained throughout the journey had done little to quell the turmoil in my own mind. The ghastly images of the previous day, seared into my memory, replayed themselves with sickening regularity, defying all attempts at suppression. I clung to Holmes' words, hoping for a momentary reprieve, a fleeting distraction from the horrors that haunted me.

I turned towards him, my attention rapt. He paused, as if gauging my readiness for what he was about to reveal, before continuing.

"You will recall, Watson that the initial reports mentioned the victim's lower body being exposed."

"Hm," I murmured, my response deliberately noncommittal. I had no desire to revisit that particular detail.

Holmes, however, seemed undeterred. His eyes, I observed, held a glint of intellectual excitement, a spark that belied the grim subject matter. While I had spent the journey attempting to banish the horrors of the crime from my mind, he had clearly been dissecting them, reconstructing the sequence of events with the meticulous precision of a watchmaker reassembling a shattered timepiece.

"And yet," he continued, his voice laced with a hint of triumph, "there was no indication of a struggle, no sign of forced entry." He paused, allowing his words to sink in. "This suggests, Watson, that the act itself, the act of intercourse, was consensual."

"The deed, I believe, would have been done directly after the fellow concluded his business. The look upon the poor woman's face, you see, and the splatter of blood upon the fence - all point to a swiftness that left her no time for comprehension, let alone resistance," Holmes mused, his voice sharp as ever.

"Savage, Holmes, positively savage!" I exclaimed, unable to contain my disgust.

"And yet, my dear Watson," Holmes countered, a hint of amusement in his tone, "have you not heard of the Black Widow spider?"

I knew, of course, the creature to which he referred - a chilling example of nature's cruelty, the female devouring her mate. I remained silent, however, allowing him to continue his line of thought.

"Man, Watson, is prone to ritual, particularly after certain... exertions. Some crave a smoke, others a restorative cup of coffee, still others succumb to slumber. And then there are those, you see, who require a different sort of indulgence, something more... intoxicating." He paused, his gaze sweeping the room. "Had our man been a devotee of the leaf, we should find evidence of it here - a scattering of cigarette ends, perhaps."

"And did you?" I inquired, my curiosity piqued. "

"No, but observe, my dear Watson, the cuttings themselves are his indulgence."

"I confess, Holmes, I am at a loss."

"Look closer! The very ferocity of the act, the sheer... enthusiasm with which it was carried out. The blood, Watson, picture it! He would have been drenched, positively bathed in it!"

"But Holmes, a man so saturated in gore - how could he vanish into the city without a trace? It lends credence to Llewellyn's ravings of evil spirits."

"Nonsense, Watson. We have established the copious nature of the bloodshed. Our man would have been well-painted, it's true, but surely not so witless as to parade about in such a state. A butcher's apron, perhaps, similar to that worn by Llewellyn himself..."

"You believe then, that this 'leather apron fellow,' as you call him, strolled through the streets thus attired? Dripping blood? My dear Holmes, even granting a modicum of practicality, surely he would have at least cleansed his hands before venturing out." then I was reminded of the garden tap I had observed during my initial investigation with Lusk, a stone's throw from the grim scene.

Holmes, with a flourish, adjusted his deerstalker cap. "Therein, my dear Watson, lies the rub."

"Pray, enlighten me."

"The blood, you see, from the wound upon her throat - it flowed down the steps, pooling where she lay. He did not move her, not an inch. Instantaneous, her demise. And our man, he would have had to step over, through that pool to make his escape. Did you, by any chance, observe a basin of water nearby? Freshly used?"

"I cannot recall..."

"Neither could I. Which suggests, rather strongly, that our man did not avail himself of such an amenity."

"Hmm," I conceded, my mind awhirl as our carriage took a turn towards Paddington. A thought struck me. "But the womb, Holmes, what of that gruesome detail?"

Holmes turned to me, his expression unreadable. "Tell me, Watson, after such an… exertion, would our man, already fatigued, truly undertake such a laborious task? The removal of an organ is no trifling matter."

"Indeed," I replied, pondering his words. "And this was no ordinary organ, but the very seat of a woman's life force."

Holmes offered no reply, his silence speaking volumes.

The week that followed saw little of Holmes at Baker Street. Each morning he would depart, smartly attired, only to return late at night, his demeanor that of a common laborer who had seen a hard day's work.

When I pressed him on the matter, he offered only, "Hunting for the Leather Apron," but in truth, that was all I needed to hear. The very phrase, I daresay, would have calmed the collective nerves of Spitalfields, of Whitechapel, of London itself. Sherlock Holmes on the prowl - ill tidings indeed for any villain foolish enough to be abroad!

Nor was Holmes alone in his pursuit. The City Police Commissioner, in a fit of somewhat misguided zeal, had unleashed a pack of hounds upon Whitechapel, hoping to sniff out the villain's trail. The endeavor proved fruitless, the dogs scattering hither and thither with no apparent rhyme or reason, and indeed, causing such consternation amongst the populace that the mayor himself was forced to call a halt to the canine patrol.

It was mid-afternoon, close to the hour of three, when Holmes presented himself at my door, clutching a bundle of papers. "A task for you, my dear Watson," he declared, thrusting the stack into my hands. "I should have brought you along."

I examined the contents - a collection of letters, penned in Holmes' own hand. He himself, I noted, appeared weary, collapsing onto the sofa with a sigh and proceeding to light his pipe.

"Turned scribe, have we, Holmes?" I remarked, unable to suppress a twinge of professional jealousy. My accounts of Holmes' exploits for The Strand were, after all, a not insignificant source of income. The thought of my friend and colleague usurping my literary endeavors was...unsettling.

"Fear not, Watson," he chuckled, "I've no intention of stealing your thunder. A mere bit of playacting, you see."

Playacting? Then it dawned on me - his whereabouts these past few days were explained.

"A journalist, I've discovered, Watson, often has more success extracting information than a mere detective. People tend to loosen their tongues when confronted with a notebook and a keen ear." He gestured towards the stack of papers. "Spitalfields, my dear fellow, disguised as a humble reporter. Lusk's advance money went towards procuring these little gems of gossip." He gestured towards the papers. "Remarkable, the things people reveal when they believe they're speaking to the press."

"Indeed, Holmes, indeed! I've often suspected as much myself. There are times I wonder if our journalistic brethren don't embellish their accounts with a touch of imagination."

"Why not see for yourself, Watson?" He leaned back, eyes closed, though I knew sleep was far from his mind. "Read me these 'secret reports,' as it were, and I'll provide any necessary clarifications."

I picked up the first letter, a sense of anticipation building within me, and began to read...

17.

Statement of Louise Wilkinson, Proprietress of the Lodging House at No. 30, Dorset Street

"Annie Chapman, she was acquainted with a man some two years ago - Jack Sivvy, they called him. I recall it clearly, for 'Sivvy' was no proper surname, but earned from his trade, a maker of such implements. Annie, as his paramour, was known then as Annie Sivvy as well. A quiet soul, she was not one for drink or boisterousness. The news of her drunken shouting that night struck me as odd, I confess. Two children she had, or so she told me. A son, afflicted, poor lad, residing in an orphanage, and a daughter, living abroad in France."

Timothy Donovan, Proprietor of the Lodging House at No. 35, Dorset Street

"The deceased, she was no stranger to my establishment. Many a night she spent under this very roof, these past four months especially. A regular habit she'd made of it. Kept to herself mostly, gave no trouble. Once, I recall, she spoke of a longing for a respectable life, like that of her kin. A wistful sigh accompanied those words. Good stock, perhaps, fallen on hard times. Never spoke of her acquaintances, though, nor their origins. Saturdays, now and then, a pensioner, perhaps, or a soldier, would accompany her, staying through Monday. That's how I remember her so clearly, you see. Recognise those men, I would, anywhere. To think, after availing themselves of her services... Unconscionable! Typically, after these men departed on Monday morning, she'd linger a day or two more. Eight pence, I charged her for the accommodation. This last time, however..."

It was here that Holmes interrupted my reading. "I inquired, Watson, as to whether he had seen her since that departure. Donovan, you see, claimed he had not laid eyes upon her from that day until Friday."

"Friday?" I echoed, startled. "This past Friday, you mean?"

"Precisely," affirmed Holmes. "Friday last, half past eleven at night, she returned to Donovan's establishment. When questioned as to her whereabouts since Monday, she claimed illness, a stay in hospital, before departing towards Bishopsgate Street."

"A fabrication, surely, Holmes! The man turned her out, the poor woman being unwell and all."

"That was my initial assumption as well, Watson. Donovan's demeanor, however... there was an evasiveness, a carefully constructed facade of sincerity. He claimed she lacked the funds for lodging, you see. Penniless."

I resumed my perusal of Holmes' notes.

"She reappeared at the lodging house around half past one in the morning, requesting a bed. My assistant, upon relaying this request, was instructed to provide lodging only if payment could be met. It was then that she uttered a curious phrase, 'Brummie, I won't be long. See if Jim can turn down a bed.' Exhaustion, rather than intoxication, seemed to be her primary affliction. She departed, munching on a baked potato. I saw no more of her until yesterday, at the mortuary, where I identified her by her curly hair and general features. It was after her departure on Monday that I discovered two bottles amongst her belongings. One bore the inscription, 'St. Bartholomew's Hospital, two tablespoons thrice daily.'"

"Donovan," interjected Holmes, "claimed to have disposed of the bottles, their contents being, in his estimation, 'poisonous.'"

"Poison?" I echoed, my brow furrowing.

"One contained a milky white cream," Holmes elaborated. "The label read, 'St. Bartholomew's Hospital. For external use only. Poison.'"

"Then her claim of illness, of medication, it was the truth!" I exclaimed.

Holmes nodded curtly. "But that, my dear Watson, is not the most intriguing detail." He sat upright, fixing me with a hawk-like stare.

I leaned forward, my curiosity piqued. "And what, pray tell, is?"

"As I turned to leave, a parting inquiry, I asked Donovan if he was acquainted with this 'Leather Apron' fellow. His response, Watson, was most unexpected. 'Know him?' he exclaimed. 'Why, I know him well!'"

18.

"Seems the fellow took up residence in Donovan's establishment some twelve months ago, accompanied by a woman he introduced as his wife. The following morning, however, cries of 'Murder!' rang through the house. Donovan and his staff, upon investigation, discovered the woman being brutally assaulted, dragged by her hair and clothing. The Leather Apron, for it was he, claimed the woman had attempted theft, justifying his savagery. Donovan, unconvinced, promptly evicted the brute. He returned several times thereafter, each time with a different female companion, but Donovan refused him lodging."

Holmes paused, drawing deeply from his pipe. "The Ten Bells public house, Watson, run by one E. Waldron, sits at the edge of Spitalfields Market, on Commercial Street. The barman there, George Suttler by name, provided some curious information regarding Annie Chapman. You'll find his statement in that stack of papers."

I located the relevant document and began to read.

"Five o'clock in the morning it was, thereabouts, when she arrived. Appearance, shall we say, was not her strong suit. Her Blouse and skirt matched awfully. Middle-aged woman like that, you'd think she'd have more sense. Anyway, a fellow, drunk as a lord, pokes his head in, demanding she join him outside. Angry sort, he was. Then, quick as a flash, he's gone, vanished. Believe he caught sight of me standing there, covered his face. Managed to get a glimpse, though, and he was wearing a hat."

"The murderer, Holmes!" I exclaimed, unable to contain my excitement. "This must be him!"

"The barman," said Holmes, a hint of disappointment in his voice, "could only recall the absence of a coat. No other distinguishing features, unfortunately. He claims, however, that he would recognize both the man and the woman should he see them again."

"Recognize them?" I echoed, bewildered. "He doesn't know, then? About Chapman's murder?"

"That's the crux of it, Watson. I escorted the fellow to the mortuary this morning, only to have him declare that the deceased was not the woman he had encountered."

"Blast! Then we haven't a witness to place the killer with Chapman!" I slumped back in my chair, deflated.

"The timing aligns, however," mused Holmes, "and the other details are consistent."

"Perhaps," I ventured, "the barman's memory is faulty? Or he found it hard to identify the body, after its time in the formalin..."

"Impossible, Watson. Another woman, present at the identification, confirmed her identity without hesitation."

I flipped through the stack of papers, eager to locate this new testimony. Holmes, however, possessed a near-photographic memory, and proceeded to recount the woman's statement verbatim. I followed along, checking for any discrepancies, but his recall was flawless.

"Amelia Farmer, her name was. She was already at the mortuary when we arrived at ten. A vital piece of information she provided, Watson. Seems she had lodged with the deceased at that very same public house, knew her quite well, in fact. According to Farmer, Chapman's husband was a veterinary surgeon, practicing in Windsor. And, mark you, he was known to wear a leather apron when attending to his patients."

"Good heavens, Holmes!" I exclaimed, unable to contain my excitement. "The very description of our killer!"

Holmes, however, did not share my enthusiasm. "Indeed, Watson. But there's more. Farmer also stated that this surgeon... had died eighteen months prior."

"Hearsay, Holmes, mere hearsay! We need confirmation, surely?"

"Precisely, my dear fellow. Was Annie Chapman's husband Jack Sivvy, the sieve maker, or this leather-aproned surgeon? Or could they be one and the same? That, Watson, is the puzzle we must solve."

"And this Farmer woman, how well did she know Chapman?"

"Well enough to identify her friend's body the moment she entered the mortuary, Watson. The shock, I daresay, was palpable. She remained rooted to the spot, overcome with grief. That's how I encountered her, you see, when I arrived with George Soul. She spoke at length about her friend's past. Seems Chapman had separated from her husband some time ago, a mutual agreement, with a settlement of ten shillings per week. The money was sent via post, arriving regularly at the Commercial Street office. Eighteen months ago, however, the payments ceased. Upon inquiry, Chapman was informed of her husband's demise. No concrete proof, mind you, just hearsay. But there were other details... or rather, the lack thereof that I found curious."

"Go on, Holmes."

"For all her reminiscing, Farmer seemed curiously uninformed about certain aspects of Chapman's life. She mentioned two children, but knew nothing of their whereabouts. Even Chapman's own parents remained vague figures, residing somewhere in Brompton or Fulham, she couldn't quite recall which."

"Curious, isn't it, how intimately acquainted she claimed to be with Chapman, merely from sharing lodgings? Some accounts suggest they were barely on speaking terms."

"Farmer, it seems, had a penchant for corresponding with friends, a habit she claimed gave her keen insight into Chapman's life. Yet, when pressed for the address of this supposed sister or mother, her memory faltered. Somewhere near Brompton Hospital, she vaguely recalled. Another time, Chapman had apparently expressed a desire to borrow her sister's boots, to go mushroom picking in the woods, to escape her...profession. And then there was mention of a brother, residing on or near Oxford Street."

"A tangled web indeed, Holmes," I remarked, my skepticism growing with each new detail. "This Farmer woman's account, it doesn't quite ring true, does it?"

"Indeed, Watson. And the inconsistencies are not merely in relation to other testimonies. Farmer contradicts even herself. She paints Chapman as a teetotaler, a woman of tranquility, yet admits to occasional bouts of drinking."

"Finding this elusive husband, Holmes, that's the key to unlocking this mystery, wouldn't you say?"

"Ah, but there's the rub, Watson. According to Farmer, there was another... a soldier by the name of Ted Stanley. Currently employed at a distillery, she claimed, and a good man, patient too. Tall fellow, fair, with a gentle disposition. She'd wager anything, she said, that Stanley wouldn't hurt a fly, let alone raise a hand to Chapman. 'Wouldn't harm her with a fingernail,' those were her very words."

I shook my head, incredulous. This Amelia Farmer, it seemed, possessed a rather fluid relationship with the truth. Holmes, meanwhile, had refilled his pipe, and now puffed away thoughtfully.

"Three rings, Watson," he remarked, a sly smile playing upon his lips. "Farmer distinctly remembers Chapman wearing three rings that Friday evening."

"Rings?" I echoed. "But if she possessed such valuables, why the inability to pay for lodging?"

His smile widened, and I realized, with a pang of self-reproach, that Holmes had grasped the significance long before I had.

"That, my dear Watson," he replied, his voice laced with amusement, "is precisely the question I posed to her."

"And her response?"

"Cheap imitations, sir," mimicked Holmes, perfectly capturing Farmer's tone.

"Yet," I pointed out, "there were no rings found on the body."

"Farmer, resourceful as ever, had an explanation at the ready. Someone, she suggested, must have mistaken the baubles for genuine articles, and in the course of attempting to pilfer them, accidentally caused Chapman's demise."

"The police, acting on her testimony, attempted to locate this supposed mother, sister, and cousin, but to no avail. A man named Chapman on Oxford Street proved to be a dead end, no relation to our victim."

Holmes threw back his head and let out a hearty laugh. "The woman's a charlatan, Watson, a downright fraud!" The sheer audacity of Farmer's fabrication, concocted under the very nose of Sherlock Holmes, no less, proved contagious, and I found myself joining in his mirth, despite the gravity of the situation.

When our laughter subsided, I turned to Holmes, my brow furrowed. "But why, Holmes? Why spin such an elaborate tale about Annie Chapman?"

"To conceal her profession, Watson."

"And what profession would that be?"

"She was, shall we say, a woman of the evening."

A moment of silence passed between us. "However, Watson," Holmes continued, his tone turning serious, "As amusing as this all seems, an incident occurred on my way home that rather dampened my spirits."

"Indeed? What happened?"

"I made a few inquiries at local pawnbrokers, you see, just to see if there was any truth to Farmer's story."

"And?"

"Unbelievable, Watson, utterly unbelievable. A man matching our description recently attempted to pawn three gold rings at a shop on Mile End Road. The pawnbroker, upon discovering their true nature, refused the transaction."

The last vestiges of our laughter evaporated. "You're suggesting, then, that Farmer... that she was telling the truth?"

"People rarely lie outright, Watson, just as they rarely tell the whole truth. It's why I place little stock in eyewitness accounts, preferring to rely on observation and deduction. I've a mind to pen a treatise on the subject, in fact."

"The day you turn author, Holmes," I chuckled, my tone light despite the surge of professional envy I felt, "is the day my own writing career faces its stiffest competition."

"Fear not, Watson," chuckled Holmes. "You shall retain your literary monopoly. Dictation, perhaps, should the urge to chronicle my methods ever strike me, but the act of writing itself holds little appeal. Far too tedious for a mind such as mine. Give me puzzles, Watson, not blank pages. Let me unravel mysteries, not sentences."

He paused, setting his pipe down with a contemplative air. "Speaking of mysteries..." He leaned forward, his gaze intent, and I instinctively mirrored his posture, sensing a revelation.

"Had that pawnbroker accepted those rings, Watson," he murmured, his voice low and conspiratorial, "we could have presented them to Farmer as irrefutable proof, convinced her they were Chapman's. A powerful piece of evidence, don't you think? Enough, perhaps, to shake her facade and lead us to the killer."

I sat back, impressed as always by Holmes' ability to find opportunity even in the most convoluted of circumstances.

It seemed, however, that Holmes had yet more to reveal from his trove of journalistic treasures. He selected another letter from the pile, placing it in my hand with a flourish.

"Another intriguing lead, my dear Watson, courtesy of Mrs. Fiddymont, wife of the proprietor of the Prince Albert public house."

"A 'clean' establishment, as they say," he elaborated, "situated at the junction of Brushfield and Stuart Streets, roughly half a mile from the scene of the crime."

"Mrs. Fiddymont reported that while engaged in conversation with another lady at the bar, around seven that morning, a man entered, his appearance most unsettling."

I located Mrs. Fiddymont's statement and began to read aloud.

"A brown bowler hat he wore, and a dark coat, but no waistcoat beneath. Pulled low over his brow, that hat was, as if to conceal his features. Covered half his face, it did. The rest, well, a thick beard saw to that. Ordered a pint of ale, he did. I caught myself studying him in the mirror behind the bar as I drew his drink. Must have noticed, for he turned sharpish, hiding himself behind a pillar, pretending not to see. But we women, we notice these things, don't we? Knew he was concealing something, so I kept my eye on him, reflecting in that glass."

"At this point, Watson," interjected Holmes, "she leaned forward, her voice hushed, and declared, 'As God is my witness, sir, my eyesight is sharp. And I saw it clear as day - bloodstains on his right hand.'"

I glanced down at the letter, confirming her words. Even knowing Holmes' remarkable memory, I couldn't help but be impressed.

But a thought struck me, a detail nagging at my memory. "The right hand, Holmes?" I interjected. "But surely our man is left-handed?"

Holmes shook his head, a hint of amusement in his eyes. "She is quite correct, Watson. The right hand, as seen in the mirror's reflection. Which, if you'll engage your considerable powers of deduction, would make the actual hand... the left. This, my dear fellow, is our man."

Of course! How could I have forgotten the simple principle of mirrored images?

Holmes tapped the paper, urging me to continue.

"He chilled me to the bone. That one did. A face only a mother could love, and even then... We hadn't heard about the poor woman, not yet. As he drank, I noticed his shirt, torn it was, ripped clean through. And the way he drank that ale, one gulp, gone! Such thirst, at that hour? Paid and hurried out, he did. I signaled to my friend with my eyes, and she followed him, discreetly, you understand. I stayed put, pretending nothing was amiss. Mrs. Mary Chapel, she's called, lives at No. 28, Stuart Street."

"I paid Mrs. Chapel a visit myself, Watson," said Holmes. "Her account corroborated Mrs. Fiddymont's in every detail."

"This is remarkable, Holmes!" I exclaimed, gripping the arms of my chair. "The pieces are falling into place!"

"Indeed," he replied, his tone laced with intrigue. "But Mrs. Chapel, it seems, had even more to add." He paused for dramatic effect. "Seems our man, sensing her scrutiny, catching her eye turned suddenly. The look he gave her, Watson... well, it frightened the poor woman so thoroughly that even Mrs. Fiddymont urged her to abandon her pursuit. But not before she observed a rather telling detail - a tattered shirtsleeve."

Holmes directed my attention to the relevant passage in his notes, resuming his pipe-smoking ritual. I devoured the words, my pulse quickening.

"A thin line of blood, I noticed, just below his right ear, running parallel to the tear in his shirt. And then, as God is my witness, I saw it - dried blood caked between his fingers. He exited the public house, and I, foolishly brave, followed him out the other door, the one he had to pass to reach the street. But the sight of that blood, it chilled me to my core. I knew then I was in over my head. As he passed, our eyes met. Sir, a look that pierced my very soul. Like gazing upon the devil himself. Never shall I forget it. I pretended, of course, that nothing was amiss, stood there as if awaiting someone. He passed without a word, and I... I swear, I could feel the heat of his presence even after he was gone. A sweltering heat, despite the cool morning air."

"I followed him as best I could, you see. Towards Bishopsgate Street he went. Told Joseph Taylor all about it, and he went after him."

"Joseph Taylor?" I inquired, curious about this new player in our drama.

"A builder by trade," explained Holmes, "residing at No. 22, Stuart Street. He, it seems, took up the pursuit, shadowing our suspect through the labyrinthine streets. At one point, finding himself abreast of the fellow, he had a clear view of him. Thinner than we imagined, Watson, and not as tall. Five foot three, perhaps, at most. Forty years of age, by the look of him."

"Black and white trousers, dotted pattern, rather too snug, by Taylor's account. Dark coat, same as before. And the smell, Watson... Taylor described it as a potent mix of unwashed body and something metallic, like the inside of an old railway carriage."

"Blood!" I exclaimed, the word escaping my lips before I could stop it. Holmes nodded curtly, but continued his narration without pause.

"As they walked side-by-side, the man turned, fixing Taylor with a stare so intense, so predatory, that Taylor likened it to a hawk's. I've no doubt the man possesses a certain animal cunning. He kept his hands clutched tightly to his coat, as if to shield himself from view. Agitated, he was, and Taylor, I daresay, felt a shiver of apprehension at that moment. A brown mustache, he noted, and close-cropped hair, though the hat obscured most of it. Not wanting to arouse suspicion, Taylor eventually veered off, but not before observing the man disappear into a rather unsavory establishment on Half Moon Street - the 'Dirty Dicks,' if you'll pardon the vulgarity."

Holmes fell silent then, lost in thought. I dared not disturb him. Was he piecing together the fragments of the case in his mind's eye, or had he succumbed to a bout of exhaustion? Deciding it best not to interrupt, I turned my attention back to the stack of papers, selecting the next statement at random. It bore the name Mrs. Bell, a resident of Hanbury Street, living in the very shadow of the crime scene. I began to read, my curiosity piqued.

Mrs. Bell, Hanbury Street.

"Lived here a good while now, I have. Wouldn't recommend it, mind you. See something like that, well, it'd shake even the strongest of women..."

"Next door, you see, it's a lodging house, always open, always someone coming and going. This poor girl, she was dragged, tortured... No doubt in my mind, the same killer responsible for the others. It was Adam Osbourne raised the alarm this morning. 'For God's sake!' he cried, 'Murder! Murder!' We all woke, threw on our clothes, rushed out. There she was, poor soul, by the stairs leading to the back court. Clothes ripped, body... well, I won't sully your ears with the details. Those in the lodging house, they slept through it all, oblivious until the police arrived. Can't say for sure if any of them were involved, but I doubt it, I truly do. That passageway, it's always open, night and day. Anyone could have slipped in, committed the awful deed, and slipped out again. Knew all the lodgers by sight, I did. None of them the type, not in a million years."

"As she surmised, Watson," added Holmes, "there was nothing in the lodgers' statements or demeanor to arouse suspicion. Nor did anyone implicate them, as I myself can attest."

I finished reading, placing the letter back on the table with a sigh. The sound seemed to rouse Holmes from his reverie. Before I could voice the question burning in my mind, however, he spoke.

"I've relayed all this to Lusk and Abberline at Scotland Yard, Watson. The rest, as they say, is in their hands."

21.

One morning, Lusk presented himself at our door, accompanied by a figure we had not anticipated encountering.

"Inspector Abberline," greeted Holmes, gesturing towards a chair. "To what do we owe this pleasure?"

"A debt of gratitude, Mr. Holmes, for the information you provided," replied Abberline, his tone courteous yet strained. "And a request for your continued assistance." I sensed, however, that this was not the full extent of his purpose. His gaze flickered towards Lusk, a distinct reluctance to speak freely in the other's presence.

Lusk, for his part, seemed equally ill at ease in Abberline's company. "A chance encounter, Mr. Holmes, I assure you," he interjected, his voice laced with forced joviality. "But be that as it may, we find ourselves united in our pursuit of justice, and you, sir, are instrumental to that end. Hence, we agreed before crossing your threshold that our shared purpose superseded any... professional friction."

I glanced at Holmes. He was not one for playing peacemaker, yet fate, it seemed, had cast him in that very role.

"Capital!" he declared, his tone betraying none of the tension that crackled in the air. "An opportunity for a meeting of minds, wouldn't you say? Pray, gentlemen, be seated. Enlighten us with your respective purposes, and let us see what common ground we might find. Transparency, I believe, is paramount."

Abberline's face remained a mask of guarded skepticism, but at Holmes' invitation, both men took seats facing each other before the fireplace. Holmes settled onto the sofa, while I remained standing, leaning against the table.

"I trust," added Holmes, "that my friend, the good doctor, doesn't present an obstacle to our discussion. His discretion, gentlemen, is as ironclad as my own."

To my surprise, both men readily agreed.

"Then allow me to commence," began Abberline, his gaze steady. "Acting upon the information you provided, Mr. Holmes, we've conducted thorough inquiries. We are now certain that our suspect is left-handed and possesses surgical knowledge. Consequently, I've ordered the release of several individuals in custody, those lacking these specific attributes. A significant narrowing of the field, wouldn't you say?"

His tone, cordial until now, turned sharp as he addressed Lusk. "Baker Street, I daresay, proves a more convenient destination than Bromley, wouldn't you agree?"

"The conduct of the provincial police leaves much to be desired, Inspector," retorted Lusk, his voice tight with disapproval. "These murders must cease, and quickly." He turned back to Holmes. "Detective Inspector MacDonald spoke highly of your expertise, Mr. Holmes. Your reputation, it seems, precedes you, even across the Atlantic."

"Mr. Lusk," interjected Holmes, his tone soothing yet firm, "while I understand your frustration, it's hardly fair to lay the failings of the constabulary at Inspector Abberline's feet. He is, I assure you, one of Scotland Yard's finest. Even without my involvement, I have no doubt he would bring this case to a successful resolution." Abberline, at this unexpected praise, allowed a flicker of gratitude to cross his features.

Lusk, to his credit, offered Abberline a curt nod. "Resolution, Mr. Holmes, is paramount, but it must come swiftly. That is why my committee and I have seen fit to engage the services of two private detectives, at our own expense."

Two? My mind raced. Did Lusk intend Holmes and myself, or was there another detective besides Holmes? Then, it dawned on me - Abberline's mention of Bromley. The second detective must reside there. Holmes, for his part, seemed not to notice, his gaze fixed intently upon his two guests.

"One thing is certain, gentlemen," he declared, his voice sharp as a honed blade. "Only through cooperation, through setting aside our differences, can we hope to see this case to its conclusion."

"An alliance most improbable," mused Abberline, as if speaking to himself.

Lusk cleared his throat, a nervous tremor in his hand as he reached for his glass. "Our surveillance efforts in Whitechapel, gentlemen, have but one objective - to apprehend this killer. There is no political agenda, no subversive intent, as some would have you believe. We are neither Marxists nor anarchists, Inspector. A misunderstanding, I assure you." He fixed Abberline with a steady gaze. "Our committee is comprised solely of concerned citizens, volunteers all, dedicated to assisting the police in their duty. We seek only to protect our community, not to incite rebellion."

Abberline's expression darkened. It was clear that Lusk was aware of the rumors circulating about his committee, whispers that had even reached the hallowed halls of Scotland Yard. I myself had never entertained such notions, always finding Lusk to be a man of integrity.

"Sixteen businessmen strong, our committee," continued Lusk, turning back to Holmes. "All respectable members of the

Whitechapel and Spitalfields community. The impact of these murders on our livelihoods is undeniable, Mr. Holmes, but I assure you. Our sole purpose is to see the perpetrator brought to justice." He paused, then added, his gaze shifting back to Abberline, "I was elected Chairman unanimously, at a meeting held on the tenth of September. George Lusk, at your service. Chairman of the Whitechapel Vigilance Committee. Our Treasurer is Joseph Aaron, a civil servant. B. Harris serves as Secretary. Our esteemed members include Messrs. Burnett, Cohen, H. Harris, Hodgins, Isaac, Houghton, Laughton, Lindsay, Michelson, Reeves, and Rogers. All businessmen, you see, representing a variety of trades - builders, tobacconists, tailors, picture-framers, shipping agents, even an actor among us. And this," he declared, producing a card from his breast pocket, "is our official documentation."

He presented the card to Abberline with a flourish. From my vantage point, I could see that it was larger, more ornate, than the one he had shown us previously. I craned my neck, peering over Abberline's shoulder, eager for a closer look.

THE WHITECHAPEL VIGILANCE COMMITTEE

Formed in response to the recent outrages committed by the Whitechapel Fiend for the purpose of apprehending the said malefactor.

CHAIRMAN
Mr Geo. Lusk

TREASURER
Mr Jos. Aarons

☞ Meetings held and all enquiries to:- ☜

The Crown Public House
74 MILE END ROAD.

Lusk launched into his account, his voice booming with conviction. Holmes pointed out the Masonic symbol emblazoned at the top - the "all-seeing eye," the square and compass - but, for the moment, remained silent, allowing Lusk to plead his case.

Abberline leaned forward, his fingers steepled thoughtfully, listening intently. He had, it seemed, decided to let Lusk speak his piece uninterrupted.

"It began, as you know, on the thirty-first of August," Lusk declared. "Mary Ann Nichols, found lifeless on Buck's Row, near the London Hospital at three forty-five in the morning, by a carter named Charles Cross. Lying there, she was, in front of those gated stables. His cries brought Constable John Neil to the spot. Her throat was slashed, a gruesome sight." He paused, his gaze hardening. "We, the citizens of Whitechapel, are dissatisfied, gentlemen, with the protection afforded us by the police."

We were all, of course, intimately familiar with the details of the case, but Abberline, like Holmes, remained silent, allowing Lusk to continue.

"Thus, we initiated our own patrols," Lusk explained. "Men of the community, out of work, carefully selected for their character. They walk the streets of East London from dusk till midnight, then again till dawn."

He sat ramrod straight, a formidable figure in his heavy coat and gloves, his thick walking stick planted firmly between his knees. I observed the prominent muscles in his neck, the powerful cords of his Sternocleidomastoid and Trapezius, straining against the confines of his collar. They spoke of a man accustomed to holding his head high, bearing the weight of responsibility like Atlas himself. The thought crossed my mind to suggest he might find some comfort in leaning back, but I refrained, sensing that this rigid posture was as much a part of his character as the words he spoke.

"We compensate these men from our own pockets," he continued. "And we, along with the police, have equipped them with whistles, rubber-soled boots, and sturdy staffs. Furthermore, every evening at nine, the full committee convenes at the Crown Club. At half past twelve, when the establishment closes, we join the patrols ourselves. Later still, the Working Men's Vigilance Committee joins the effort."

I sensed a flicker of something in Abberline's eyes, a desire to speak, but still he held his tongue. Holmes, too, seemed to notice. His gaze darted from Lusk to Abberline, then finally settled on me, as if gauging my reaction. I shook my head subtly, wanting no part in this volatile game of cat and mouse.

"It speaks poorly of London, that a man of Mr. Lusk's stature should feel compelled to seek assistance outside the established channels," declared Holmes, his voice laced with a hint of reproof. He gestured towards Lusk, his expression a mixture of sympathy and disapproval. "That the citizenry should feel the need to take the law into their own hands speaks volumes about the perceived efficacy of the police force." He paused, his gaze softening as he addressed Lusk directly. "However, sir, I must reiterate my conviction that Inspector Abberline represents the very best of Scotland Yard. Let us not, I implore you, tar him with the same brush as those less... capable." He turned to me, his eyebrow raised in question. "Wouldn't you agree, Watson?"

I nodded my assent, and Lusk, after a moment's hesitation, followed suit. A ghost of a smile flickered across Abberline's face.

Holmes then turned his attention to the Inspector. "This metropolis, this heart of an empire upon which the sun never sets, it deserves a more... elevated class of criminal," he mused, his voice tinged with a hint of wistful irony. "My skills and my intellect, were honed to match wits with masterminds, not to contend with this current plague of common thugs and cutthroats." He paused, fixing Abberline with a penetrating stare. "You would agree, I trust, Inspector?"

22.

"The entirety of the constabulary, Mr. Holmes, now operates under my direct authority," stated Abberline, his gaze unwavering. "You need have no further concerns on that front. I've made it abundantly clear that the law must be applied equally, without fear or favor." His words were directed at Holmes, yet it was evident that they were intended for Lusk's ears, and the latter seemed to take some comfort in the Inspector's assertion.

Abberline, however, was not quite finished. He leaned forward, fixing Holmes with a keen eye. "Now then, Mr. Holmes, perhaps you'd be so kind as to share the pressing news I believe you've been holding back."

It dawned on me then that Abberline's presence was no mere courtesy call. Holmes had orchestrated this meeting, this unlikely alliance, for a specific purpose.

He leaned towards his two guests, his voice dropping to a conspiratorial murmur. "Gentlemen, you should know that it's not my habit to divulge suspicions or deductions before a case is solved, before every lead has been meticulously verified. My friend, Dr. Watson, will attest to that." He paused, letting the gravity of his next words sink in. "However, circumstances, as they so often do, necessitate a certain flexibility. To stop this killer, or killers, we must pool our resources, share our insights. That, gentlemen, is why I requested your presence today. To lay bare my doubts."

His voice had dropped to a near whisper, compelling me to draw closer to catch his words. Lusk remained ramrod straight, but his eyes gleamed with anticipation. Abberline, unable to contain his curiosity, leaned in further still.

"You are both aware, I presume, of my methods," began Holmes, his voice low and steady. "Observation and deduction are my tools, and through them, I glean insights into the criminal mind from the very scenes of their crimes. These murders are no different. The devil, gentlemen, is in the details."

He paused, letting the weight of his words settle before continuing. "Consider the Nichols case. Buck's Row, where the unfortunate woman met her end, lies a stone's throw from London Hospital. A significant number of patients being treated there, I've discovered, suffer from a rather... delicate affliction. Syphilis, to be precise. The hospital even maintains a separate ward for such cases."

"Now, I ask you to consider this: why would our killer choose to strike so close to a hospital renowned for treating this particular ailment?" His gaze swept across our faces, challenging us to follow his line of reasoning. "These women, these unfortunate souls who ply their trade on the streets, they are, shall we say, vectors of this disease. They, along with most migrant workers, congregate in the vicinity of the hospital at most times."

"From this, gentlemen, we can deduce a rather unsettling possibility: our killer himself may be afflicted with syphilis." He paused again, allowing the implications to sink in. "It is, after all, a disease largely confined to certain strata of society, particularly here in the East End. And as you know, there is, as yet, no known cure. To be diagnosed with syphilis, gentlemen, is to be handed a death sentence, a slow and agonizing decline into madness and ultimately, oblivion."

"Imagine, if you will, the rage, the despair that such a diagnosis would evoke. Our killer, upon learning his fate, might very well lash out at those he perceives as responsible for his condition. Picture him, gentlemen, leaving the hospital in a fit of anger and frustration, his mind ablaze with thoughts of vengeance. Who does he encounter first? Mary Ann Nichols, a woman of the night, standing on a street corner just outside the very institution that confirmed his doom. An easy target, wouldn't you say, for a man consumed by rage and despair?"

Detective Abberline pondered Holmes' words, a thoughtful frown creasing his brow. After a moment, he offered a slow nod. "Plausible, Mr. Holmes, certainly plausible. A man driven to desperation by such a diagnosis might well commit such an act. However," he countered, "the presence of surgical instruments on him, suggests a level of premeditation that doesn't quite align with a crime of passion."

George Lusk, however, seemed to harbor a different concern. "The second murder, Mr. Holmes," he interjected, his brow furrowed. "Annie Chapman, slain on Hanbury Street, a good mile from the hospital. That hardly fits your theory, does it?"

"True," conceded Holmes, "the first murder may well have been a crime of opportunity, fueled by a potent cocktail of rage and despair. But consider this: the act itself, the shedding of blood, can become intoxicating. The killer's anger, his hatred, it festers, amplified by the knowledge of his own slow demise. Each new victim becomes a release, a gruesome testament to his suffering. And gentlemen," he added, his voice dropping to a chilling whisper, "unless we stop him, this cycle of violence will only escalate. He will become addicted to the very act of killing."

Lusk, seemingly reassured, cleared his throat and rejoined the conversation. "Like Nichols, Chapman was a woman of a similar age, eking out a living on the streets. Her throat, too, was slashed." He paused, his brow furrowing as he recalled the gruesome details. "They found her body in the early morning hours, near the back entrance of a house on Hanbury Street. Seems she'd been out seeking clients, hoping to earn enough to pay her rent. The postmortem revealed a particularly disturbing detail: her abdomen had been sliced open, and... And her womb was missing. The removal of this specific organ, gentlemen, defies explanation."

"The sheer brutality of these acts," interjected Abberline, his voice grave, "it calls to mind a case from centuries past. Gilles de Rais, a French nobleman, tried and executed some four hundred years ago. Like our Whitechapel fiend, he preyed upon the innocent, though his victims were young boys, not women. And like this killer, his methods were chillingly efficient, his crimes bafflingly difficult to solve."

"An astute observation, Abberline, most astute!" exclaimed Holmes, his eyes gleaming with macabre fascination. "I'd sensed a certain resonance myself. The parallels between our Whitechapel murderer and Gilles de Rais are indeed striking. And if history is any indication, this does not bode well."

"Forty boys, by some accounts," added Abberline, his voice barely a whisper.

My jaw dropped. I'd never heard of this Gilles de Rais, and my astonishment must have been evident, for both Holmes and Abberline turned to look at me.

"As the Inspector mentioned, Watson," explained Holmes, "both killers exhibited a chilling specificity in their choice of victims. Gilles de Rais sought out young boys; our Whitechapel monster, women of the night. Furthermore, both employed a level of savagery that sets them apart from common murderers. Gilles de Rais was said to have tortured his victims before ending their lives through decapitation. Our killer, too, seems driven to mutilate, to destroy."

"Serial killers, Watson," he continued, his voice taking on a lecturing tone, "often leave their signature, a calling card that sets their work apart. The removal of the womb, I believe, is our killer's mark."

"My concern, gentlemen," interjected Abberline, his gaze grave, "is that these murders, given their sensational nature, will become grist for the rumor mill, just as the crimes of Gilles de Rais did in his time. Public fear, fueled by speculation and hearsay, can lead to unrest, to a loss of faith in the authorities. People begin to take the law into their own hands." His gaze settled on Lusk, a pointed silence hanging in the air. Lusk, however, seemed unperturbed, his expression more one of grim understanding than offense. Indeed, Abberline's words seemed less an accusation than a confession of shared anxieties.

Lusk, his gaze unwavering, fixed upon Holmes. "Why, Mr. Holmes," he pressed, "why the wombs?"

"The womb, my dear Lusk," replied Holmes, his voice soft yet edged with a hint of steel, "is the very essence of womanhood, the source of life itself. It is what gives a woman value."

"Indeed," conceded Lusk, "but that does not explain its removal. What use has this fiend for such a thing?"

Lusk's intense stare seemed to bore into Holmes, demanding an answer. Holmes, in turn, glanced at me, then at Abberline, but our silence spoke volumes. None of us, it seemed, had a satisfactory explanation for this gruesome detail. The question, unanswered, hung heavy in the smoke-filled air of the room.

Holmes, after a long moment, released a weary sigh.

"A souvenir, Lusk," interjected Abberline, his voice firm. "A memento. He takes it as a trophy, a grim reminder of his handiwork."

Lusk and I exchanged glances, both finding Abberline's explanation chillingly plausible. Holmes, however, merely nodded slowly, his brow furrowed in thought. It was clear that his mind was traveling down a different path, exploring avenues hidden from our view.

"To understand a criminal mind," continued Abberline, his gaze fixed on Lusk, "one must learn to think like a criminal." He turned to Holmes, his expression earnest. "These souvenirs, these gruesome trophies, serve a purpose beyond mere possession. They evoke the memory of the act, rekindle the thrill, the power that the killer experienced. It's a tangible link to the victim, a way to relive the deed."

Holmes, saying nothing, paced slowly across the room, his pipe clenched between his teeth. He packed the bowl with meticulous care, struck a match, and puffed thoughtfully for a moment before finally speaking.

"I won't dispute your logic, Abberline," he conceded, his voice measured. "It's a sound deduction, based on the available evidence. And yet..." He paused, his eyes taking on a distant look. "Something about this, the very specificity of the organ taken, suggests a deeper meaning, a significance beyond the merely macabre. What that might be, however..." He trailed off, shaking his head slightly.

"Whatever the reason, Mr. Holmes," interjected Lusk, his tone laced with frustration, "these brutal slayings of women, they've cast a pall over our entire city. The newspapers, as is their wont, are having a field day, sensationalizing every detail. Whitechapel is becoming synonymous with fear, with depravity. We must stop this madman before he strikes again, before the public loses all faith in the ability of the authorities to protect them." He paused, his gaze hardening. "The press has already linked Chapman's murder to Nichols', and they won't hesitate to fan the flames of hysteria with each new victim."

Lusk's demeanor softened, and he turned to Abberline, his voice laced with sincerity. "I sought Mr. Holmes' assistance not solely due to the shortcomings of the local constabulary, though their lack of progress is a source of considerable frustration, I confess." He met Abberline's gaze directly. "The longer this fiend remains at large, the more our fair city, and particularly our corner of it, suffers. I believe, Inspector, that you are a man of reason, a man who understands the gravity of our situation. We must stop these killings, by any means necessary."

Lusk then turned towards Holmes, his expression earnest. "Your reputation precedes you, Mr. Holmes. They say there is no criminal mind too cunning, no organization too vast, for you to unravel." He paused, his gaze shifting back to Abberline, a flicker of desperation in his eyes. "Inspector, for the sake of our community, I implore you, help us stop this madness."

Abberline, his face softening, extended his hand towards Lusk. "You appear to be a man of compassion, Mr. Lusk," he said, his voice surprisingly gentle. "Such qualities are all too rare in this world. Rest assured, with your assistance, and with Mr. Holmes' keen mind on the case, we will see this through."

Lusk accepted Abberline's hand, a flicker of genuine warmth crossing his features. Holmes, observing this unlikely truce from the sidelines, allowed a small smile to play upon his lips as he puffed thoughtfully on his pipe.

"You have my word, Mr. Lusk," Abberline continued, his eyes reflecting his sincerity. "We will find this killer."

As they prepared to depart, Lusk, in a gesture of newfound camaraderie, offered Abberline a lift back to the Whitechapel station in his private carriage. Abberline accepted, and the two men departed, their earlier animosity seemingly forgotten.

I closed the door behind them and turned to Holmes, who had resumed his position by the fire. I settled into my usual chair, my mind still reeling from the events of the past hour.

"Astonishing, Holmes," I remarked, shaking my head in disbelief. "To think, those two, at odds just moments ago, now riding off together like old friends. A remarkable coincidence, wouldn't you say?"

Holmes, without taking his eyes from the swirling smoke, merely chuckled. "Coincidence, my dear Watson?" he murmured, his voice laced with amusement. "I assure you, there was nothing coincidental about their simultaneous arrival. I believe in precision, in timing, particularly when orchestrating a meeting of the minds. Let's just say I have a certain talent for persuasive telegrams."

23.

Some days later, Inspector Abberline reappeared at Baker Street, this time unannounced, without the prompting of telegram or invitation. He carried with him a thick file.

"A matter I'd value your opinion on, Mr. Holmes," he stated, presenting the file to my friend.

As Holmes opened it, I caught a glimpse of handwritten letters within. Intriguing.

While Holmes perused the documents, Abberline, seemingly eager to fill the silence, offered a piece of information entirely unrelated to the file's contents.

"Acting on your suggestion, Mr. Holmes, Charles Warren, the Commissioner, has granted us permission to employ the services of a bloodhound in our investigation. As a result, constables, accompanied by the canine, patrolled Whitechapel, focusing on the areas most frequented by our quarry."

The deflation in Abberline's voice spoke volumes. "The creature proved more of a hindrance than a help, I'm afraid," he admitted, a rueful smile touching his lips. "Caused quite a stir amongst the populace. We were forced to abandon the endeavor."

"A pity," remarked Holmes, his gaze still fixed upon the letters. "Properly handled, a bloodhound can be an invaluable asset. Still, one must adapt. Tell me, Inspector, what other developments have you unearthed?"

"These letters, Mr. Holmes," inquired Abberline, his curiosity piqued, "are they from the murderer himself?"

"Patience, my dear Abberline, patience," replied Holmes, holding up the file. "These require careful study, meticulous analysis. A few days, perhaps, and I shall have a more informed opinion."

Abberline, after a moment's contemplation, nodded curtly. He retrieved his hat from the table, settling it firmly upon his head. "A telegram, then, Mr. Holmes, should you discover anything of import." With that, he took his leave.

Holmes spent the remainder of the day, and indeed, the next several days, poring over the letters, comparing their script, their phrasing, occasionally nodding off amongst them, only to rouse himself and resume his scrutiny. His dedication to the task was remarkable, almost obsessive.

Finally, unable to contain my curiosity any longer, I ventured to inquire about his singular focus. "Holmes," I began, "these letters... why such intense concentration?"

His reaction suggested he'd been anticipating my question. He selected a handful of the letters, presenting them to me with a dramatic flourish. "These missives, Watson, these supposed confessions sent to the newspapers, are fabrications! Every last one!"

He offered me his magnifying glass, a mischievous glint in his eye.

I settled by the window, taking the proffered lens, and began to examine the letters myself. Lacking Holmes' preternatural powers of observation, I found myself at a loss. How, I wondered, did he discern the falsehoods hidden within these seemingly innocuous scribbles? His eye for detail, his ability to dissect and analyse, was a gift truly extraordinary. I, alas, could only stare at the letters, their secrets hidden from my less perceptive gaze.

"A forgery, Watson, plain as day," declared Holmes, his voice crisp and certain. "But a little exercise for your powers of observation wouldn't go amiss. Assume, for the sake of argument, that these letters are genuine. Tell me, what do you see?"

"If genuine," I mused, turning the letter over in my hands, "the question becomes, who penned it?" The crimson ink, I noted, was particularly vibrant.

I attempted to emulate Holmes' deductive process, searching for clues within the script itself. One detail, in particular, struck me as significant.

"An American, Holmes!" I exclaimed, my voice ringing with newfound confidence.

Holmes nodded, a hint of a smile playing upon his lips. "Precisely, Watson. The salutation, 'Dear Boss' - no Englishman would employ such a vulgar Americanism."

"And further," I added, emboldened by my initial success, "the phrase 'it's been made right.' Another distinctly transatlantic turn of phrase."

"Indeed, Watson, indeed," chuckled Holmes. "Now, observe the paper itself. The quality, the handwriting. What can you deduce from these?"

"The script is light, the paper pristine," I noted, examining the sheet closely. "This is no labourer's hand, Holmes. Our writer is not accustomed to physical toil."

"You're on the right track, Watson. Pray, continue."

"The paper, as I said, is of superior quality," I mused, running my fingers across its smooth surface. "And the handwriting speaks of a practiced hand, a skilled penman. A scribe, perhaps. Or..." A sudden thought struck me. "Good heavens, Holmes! A journalist!"

"Excellent, Watson, excellent!" Holmes beamed, clearly pleased with my progress.

"Now, let me add a few observations of my own," he continued, taking the letter back from me. "Feel the paper, Watson, gently. Can you detect the faint indentations, the impressions of heavier writing on the sheets that lay atop this one?"

I did as instructed, though my less sensitive fingertips failed to discern the subtle embossing. Still, I nodded, unwilling to admit my deficiency. Holmes, taking the letter back, resumed his examination, his magnifying glass tracing the lines of script as he elaborated.

"Given these observations, Watson, it's highly probable that our scribe had other papers beneath this one, upon which he'd previously been writing. The pressure of his pen would have left subtle indentations, ghostly impressions that might reveal further clues. A gentle rubbing with a pencil, perhaps, could bring them to light. A name, a date, even a stray word – anything that might point us towards the author."

"What truly baffles me, Watson," he continued, his voice tinged with exasperation, "is that such a rudimentary technique seems to have escaped the notice of the police." His tone suggested he already suspected the culprit's identity.

"But Holmes," I interjected, a sudden realisation dawning, "this writer... he's not our murderer, is he? The details don't align."

Holmes nodded, his eyes gleaming with a mixture of amusement and something akin to anticipation. "Indeed, Watson. We could, of course, confirm the writer's identity by comparing this script to other samples of his handwriting." He paused, a mischievous smile spreading across his face. "Or... we could try something a bit more audacious."

"Audacious?" I echoed, intrigued.

"We could, my dear fellow, enlist the help of the very newspaper that received this missive," he chuckled, his voice laced with a hint of glee. "Publish a facsimile of the letter, along with a detailed description of the handwriting, and invite the public to assist in identifying the author. A reward offered, perhaps, to sweeten the pot." He threw back his head and let out a hearty laugh.

My brow furrowed in confusion. His plan, though ingenious, seemed fraught with potential pitfalls. He elaborated several days later.

"I already proposed, Watson, that the newspaper print a copy of the letter, along with a thorough analysis of the handwriting, in every edition across Britain. A nationwide search, if you will. Readers were to be encouraged to compare the script to any they recognised, with a handsome reward offered for information leading to the writer's identification. Lusk even agreed to contribute to the prize money."

"And?" I prompted.

"The editors, alas, declined," he sighed, his voice tinged with disappointment. "A missed opportunity, Watson. Imagine the combined efforts of millions, all working to solve this case."

He shook his head, a wry smile touching his lips. "The letter received on the twenty-fifth of September, Watson, was signed 'Jack the Ripper.' The name, it seems, has become a rather effective marketing tool for the newspapers."

"I can't argue with that," I conceded.

"He calls himself 'Ripper' due to the nature of his mutilations, not because it's his actual name," Holmes mused, his voice taking on a speculative tone. "Which further reinforces my belief that the letter is a forgery, penned by someone seeking to capitalise on the public's morbid fascination. A journalist, most likely."

"Surely, Holmes, it wouldn't be difficult for you to compare the handwriting of the various reporters and identify the culprit."

Holmes chuckled, his silence speaking volumes. It was clear that he relished the challenge, the prospect of unmasking the charlatan who dared to play such a ghoulish game.

Abberline returned some days later, his face grim, clutching another bundle of letters. "Those blasted journalists, Holmes!" he exclaimed, his voice tight with anger. "They're as bad as the murderer himself!"

I stared at him, bewildered. What connection could these newspapermen possibly have to the gruesome events unfolding in Whitechapel? Abberline's accusation, and its target, were equally baffling.

"Look at this, Holmes," he continued, thrusting the letters towards my friend. "Nothing but sensationalism, designed to inflame public opinion. Not a shred of useful information amongst them."

"With each passing day in September, the murders grow more frequent, more brutal," he added, his voice laced with a mixture of frustration and fear. "It's becoming impossible to contain the hysteria, the morbid fascination with these crimes. The newspapers, they're like vultures, circling over a carcass, each vying for the most lurid details."

"I understand your frustration, Abberline," replied Holmes, his tone calm and measured. "However, there's a possibility, however slim, that amongst these fabrications, a genuine communication from the killer himself might be lurking. And if that's the case, my dear fellow, I assure you that he's unwittingly signed his own death warrant."

24.

I don't recall a time when my friend, Sherlock Holmes, was more deeply entangled in the clutches of cocaine than during that bleak September of 1888. The continued elusiveness of the Whitechapel murderer, despite the wealth of information Holmes had provided, seemed to weigh heavily upon him. He refused all other cases, his mind, as he put it, "in a state of revolt" from lack of stimulation. He craved a problem, a puzzle that would tax his considerable intellect to its limits.

His nocturnal wanderings during this period remained shrouded in mystery. Whether he pursued the killer through the fog-choked streets or sought solace in the oblivion offered by the insidious white powder, I could not say. He volunteered no information, and I, sensing his dark mood, dared not inquire. A strange silence had fallen over London, a silence I now recognize as the ominous calm before the storm.

I was preparing for church on Sunday, the thirtieth of September, when a telegram arrived, its contents jolting me to the core.

Come at once. Commercial Street Police Station. Lusk.

The missive, arriving so early in the morning, left me little time for deliberation. Holmes was nowhere to be found, so I set off alone, my mind racing with apprehension. Lusk's summons had specified the main police station on Commercial Street. Holmes' late-night excursions these past few days had led me to believe he was laying a trap for the killer, but clearly, something had gone awry.

Resolving to respond to Lusk's summons without delay, I hailed a cab and made my way to the station. Upon arrival, however, Lusk was nowhere to be seen. Instead, it was our acquaintance from Scotland Yard, Detective Inspector Abberline, who greeted me, his face etched with a grimness I'd never witnessed before. Abberline, despite his quiet, almost bureaucratic demeanour, was the central figure in this unfolding drama.

"A dark day, Watson, a dark day indeed," he began, his voice heavy with foreboding. "A double murder, you see. Two women, slaughtered in a single night. And your friend, Holmes... he's been arrested."

The words struck me like a physical blow. Two murders! And Holmes in custody! It felt as though the world had tilted on its axis. My head swam, and I grasped the back of a nearby chair for support.

Abberline, his face a mask of weariness and frustration, gestured towards a seat. "Come, Watson, sit down."

He stared into the distance as he spoke, his gaze unfocused, as if grappling with a puzzle he couldn't quite solve. "I confess, Watson, I'm at a loss. With all that's transpired, I'm half-tempted to believe there's some unholy force at work in Whitechapel."

"Holmes arrested?" I croaked, my throat dry with fear. "But... but why? You know he has nothing to do with these murders, Abberline!"

"A misunderstanding, Doctor, I assure you," replied Abberline, his voice laced with fatigue. "I arrived on the scene as soon as the news reached me. It was I who instructed the local constabulary to enforce the law to the letter, you see. No preferential treatment, regardless of reputation. But now, I understand Lusk's frustration with our system. The officer in charge insists on the presence of a guardian before granting bail. Bureaucracy, Watson, at its most infuriating."

I struggled to comprehend his words, my mind still reeling from the shock of Holmes' arrest. "Burner Street, Watson," Abberline continued, his voice taking on an urgent tone. "You must go there, with Holmes. I don't trust anyone in this matter, not my superiors, not my subordinates. Holmes, he can help me, I know he can."

With that, he clapped his hat upon his head, offered a curt nod, and departed, leaving me alone with my swirling thoughts and a growing sense of dread.

"Your friend awaits," a gruff voice announced from within the station. A portly, elderly man, resplendent in the uniform of the Metropolitan Police, emerged, a disconcerting smile plastered across his face. It was a smile not of courtesy, but of thinly veiled contempt.

"Chief Inspector Edmund Reid," he announced, his tone laced with self-importance. "Officer in Charge of H Division, Whitechapel. All policing matters within this district fall under my purview. Dr. Watson, I presume?" He advanced towards me, his manner devoid of any pretence of respect.

Despite the horrors unfolding within his jurisdiction, Reid's ego seemed remarkably intact. It was, I confess, quite astonishing. A man of conscience, surely, would be consumed by shame at such a string of unsolved atrocities. Yet here stood Reid, radiating an air of smug self-satisfaction. It was beyond comprehension. His incompetence, his bungling of the investigation, the whispers of tampered evidence and a lack of basic detective skills, had necessitated Abberline's intervention. I suspected that Reid's inflated ego, rather than any lack of ability, was the true obstacle to capturing the killer. Holmes, just the previous day, had lamented the loss of crucial evidence due to Reid's misguided interference.

"Where is Mr. Sherlock Holmes?" I inquired, my voice tight with anxiety.

"Inspector Abberline has requested his release on bail," replied Reid, his tone condescending. "Were it not for his intervention, you'd be waiting until morning for a court appearance."

"What has happened?" I pressed. "Where is my friend?"

"Fetch the prisoner," Reid barked at a nearby constable, his voice dripping with disdain.

It was then that the full horror of the situation dawned upon me. Holmes was in a cell.

Before I could voice further questions, Reid gestured towards a chair, his manner imperious. This was his domain, and I, it seemed, was at his mercy. I sat down, my heart pounding in my chest.

"Lusk's statement indicates that your friend was engaged in some sort of charade, at his behest," Reid continued, his voice laced with disapproval. "And while Inspector Abberline has requested his release, these are serious matters, Doctor. Matters for the courts. Still, I can't simply let him walk free. Procedures must be followed, regulations adhered to. Accountability, you see, to those above me. A guardian must sign the bail documents."

A constable led Holmes into the room, his wrists bound by handcuffs. At Reid's command, the restraints were removed.

"Sign here, Holmes," Reid instructed, his tone brusque.

I glanced at Holmes, his face flushed with anger. I signaled for him to remain calm, and with a trembling hand, signed the proffered document. Holmes, his jaw clenched, added his own signature beneath mine.

"What happened, Holmes?" I asked, turning to my friend as he sat beside me, his face a mask of barely suppressed fury. It was Reid, however, who answered, his voice dripping with sarcasm.

"Ha! Your friend chose a most opportune night for his little escapade, Doctor. In fact, he should be thanking us. Had he not been in custody, I'd have arrested him this morning on suspicion of murder." He punctuated his words with bursts of laughter, clearly relishing Holmes' predicament.

Holmes' jaw clenched, the muscles in his temples pulsing. Reid, oblivious or simply uncaring, continued his narrative.

"Quite a commotion on Dorset Street last night, you see. Our constables were called to break up a brawl. Four women, engaged in a most unseemly public display. Prostitutes, all of them, no shame whatsoever. Seems one of them had encroached on the others' territory, threatening their livelihood." He glanced at Holmes, a smirk playing upon his lips.

"The fight, Doctor, it was quite the spectacle. Footwear flying, handbags flailing, limbs entangled in a most ungainly manner." He erupted into a fit of laughter, his ample belly shaking, before dissolving into a coughing fit.

"Being as it was within our jurisdiction," he continued, once he'd regained his composure, "we charged them all with disturbing the peace and took them into custody. It's a dangerous world for women these days, Doctor. This 'Leather Apron' fellow has them all on edge. Many carry weapons for protection. Can't say I blame them." His jovial demeanour vanished momentarily, replaced by a flicker of genuine concern.

"However," he continued, his voice hardening, "those who carry weapons must be disarmed before being incarcerated. The first three women surrendered theirs willingly enough, though we searched them thoroughly, just to be sure. But the fourth, ah, she proved to be a bit more resistant. Refused to be searched. A delicate situation, you see. Can't very well have a male constable searching a female prisoner. We nearly had to call in a female officer from another division. A rare breed, those. None stationed nearby, unfortunately. So, there we were, faced with the prospect of forcibly searching this recalcitrant woman, without the proper protocol."

He paused, fixing me with a triumphant smirk. "And that, Doctor, is where your friend comes in."

"This... this stubborn, foolish woman," he gestured towards Holmes, his voice dripping with sarcasm, "is your friend, Mr. Sherlock Holmes."

"You should have seen him, Doctor," chimed in the constable, a broad grin splitting his face. "Skirt, shawl, even a flowery hat. Quite the picture he made." He handed me a bag containing Holmes' confiscated attire.

I peered inside, but the constable, eager to share the details of Holmes' humiliation, continued his account.

"A veil, too, Doctor, draped artfully over the brim of that ridiculous hat. And beneath the outer garments, two flannel petticoats, layered for warmth, I suppose. And to complete the ensemble, a bustle, no less! Designed, I imagine, to give 'her' a more womanly figure. Full bust, nipped-in waist, ample hips – the whole nine yards."

"Inspector Reid," I interjected, my patience wearing thin, "what exactly are the charges against my friend?" It was clear that Holmes was being held on some flimsy pretext.

"Well, Doctor," chuckled Reid, "upon closer inspection, our 'suspicious woman' turned out to be a man in disguise. A rather convincing disguise, I'll grant you, but a man nonetheless. Caused quite a stir amongst the lads, it did." He roared with laughter, and the assembled constables, eager to please their superior, joined in the merriment.

"Never happened before in all my years on the force," Reid wheezed, wiping tears from his eyes. "Front page news, this will be, mark my words." It was clear, even to my less perceptive eye, that the police harboured a deep-seated resentment towards Holmes, a mixture of jealousy and professional envy.

Holmes' face was a mask of humiliation and anger. His elaborate ruse, it seemed, had backfired spectacularly.

"The charge, Doctor, is 'disorderly conduct while intoxicated and disguised as a female,'" Reid announced, his voice regaining its official tone. "I intended to hold him overnight for a court appearance in the morning. However, given Mr. Lusk's statement and Inspector Abberline's persuasion, I've agreed to grant bail."

Holmes, his voice tight with suppressed fury, attempted to explain that his inebriation had been feigned, a necessary part of his plan to infiltrate the criminal underworld and unmask the Whitechapel murderer. But Reid, his face contorted in another paroxysm of laughter, seemed not to hear, his ample belly shaking with mirth.

25.

We departed the station, the taste of injustice still bitter on our tongues.

"Burner Street, Watson," declared Holmes, his voice regaining its usual crispness the moment we stepped outside. "Abberline wants us there at once," I said. A thoughtful frown creased his brow. "He's a better man than we give him credit for, that Abberline. I suspect he feels this debacle even more keenly than we do."

We arrived at Burner Street to find a scene of palpable fear and unrest. The Whitechapel murderer's reign of terror had cast a long shadow over East London, but this morning, following the discovery of two murdered women in a single night, the city seemed gripped by a collective hysteria reminiscent of the days of the French Revolution. Our hired carriage navigated slowly through the throngs of anxious citizens, their faces etched with fear and suspicion. The atmosphere was thick with tension, a palpable sense of dread hanging heavy in the air.

Reaching Burner Street, we found a considerable crowd gathered, their morbid curiosity drawing them to the grim spectacle. Walking towards the scene of the crime, flanked by Inspector Abberline and Mr. Lusk, with the added protection of several constables, felt strangely theatrical, as if we were actors taking the stage before an expectant audience.

The first victim lay near a doorway, her lifeless body sprawled in a pool of congealed blood. She had been discovered in the early hours of the morning, around one o'clock, on this very Sunday, the thirtieth of September. Unlike the previous victims, her body bore no signs of mutilation, save for the fatal gash across her throat. The swift, precise cut to her jugular vein had brought about a mercifully quick demise.

The metallic tang of blood hung heavy in the air. I stepped back, allowing Holmes to examine the body undisturbed. Lusk, meanwhile, attempted to placate the agitated crowd, while Abberline, with the assistance of his constables, maintained order and took statements from witnesses.

After a thorough examination, Holmes rejoined us, his face grim. Abberline and Lusk, eager for his assessment, hurried over.

"A packet of sugared cashews, gentlemen," Holmes announced, holding up a small, crumpled bag. "Clutched tightly in her left hand. Which suggests our killer gave her no time to react, no opportunity to defend herself. The throat wound, though fatal, lacks the precision of the previous murders. I suspect our man was interrupted. Perhaps by someone leaving the music hall across the street, or by someone approaching from further down the road. Most likely, it was the arrival of the person who discovered the body."

Abberline nodded, his expression thoughtful. "A carter named Louis Diemschutz, Mr. Holmes. Your theory holds water. The carter's arrival likely startled the killer, preventing him from carrying out his usual ritual. Hence, the absence of mutilation. He was disturbed almost immediately after the deed was done."

"If that's the case," mused Lusk, glancing around the dimly lit street, "the killer must have been close by when the carter arrived. He could have easily slipped away in the darkness."

"We conducted a thorough search of the area," Abberline confirmed, his voice tinged with frustration, "but to no avail. I initially suspected some connection to the Socialist International Society, whose meeting was held nearby, but our inquiries yielded nothing concrete. And as for the local residents..." He gestured towards the surrounding houses, his expression sceptical. "None of them fit the profile."

"What about witness statements?" inquired Holmes, his eyes sharp and alert. "Have any of those proved fruitful?"

"The victim has been identified as Elizabeth Stride," replied Abberline. "Some claim she was a widow, others that she was separated from her husband. But there's one detail that everyone agrees on."

"And that is?" I prompted.

"She was, shall we say, a member of the unfortunate class," Abberline stated, his voice dropping slightly.

"I've already dispatched constables to trace her movements prior to the murder," he continued. "She left her lodgings in Spitalfields on Saturday evening, between six and seven o'clock. Said nothing about meeting anyone in particular. We have no further information about her whereabouts until, well, until she was found here."

26.

Our next destination was Mitre Square, the scene of the second murder.

It was nearing nine o'clock by the time we arrived. A more direct route, through the less congested Commercial Street, would have shaved some time off our journey, but our driver, seemingly unfazed by the urgency of our mission, navigated the crowded streets at a leisurely pace. I gazed out the carriage window, observing the faces of the passersby, their expressions ranging from morbid curiosity to outright fear. Even in our shared silence, the tension within the carriage was palpable.

Unlike the first victim, this poor woman had suffered the full brunt of the killer's depravity.

Her body, discovered shortly before three o'clock that morning, lay slumped against a wall in Mitre Square, on the northwest side, near Aldgate. The scene was one of unspeakable horror. Her throat had been savagely slashed, her face mutilated beyond recognition. And, as was the killer's gruesome signature, her abdomen had been ripped open, her entrails spilling out onto the cobblestones beside her.

"We've established the time of death with some accuracy," Abberline's voice broke through my reverie. "The constable on patrol passed this spot just before half past one. He returned at a quarter to two. The body was discovered shortly thereafter. The murder, and the subsequent mutilation, occurred within that narrow window."

Holmes knelt beside the body, his keen eyes scanning the gruesome details. Abberline crouched beside him, his expression a mixture of fascination and revulsion.

"The incisions," Holmes observed, his voice low and clinical, "were made by a skilled hand, someone with anatomical knowledge. But our man was working in haste. Notice the roughness of the cuts, compared to those on Annie Chapman's body." He indicated the jagged edges of the wounds, and both Abberline and I leaned closer, our stomachs churning. Lusk, however, remained at a distance, his face pale and drawn.

"The victim's clothing, gentlemen, may be our best hope for identification," Holmes continued, pointing to a small, distinctive pattern on the fabric. "And note this, if you will – a piece missing from her apron. Not torn in the struggle, mind you, but deliberately cut away."

"Why would he do that, Holmes?" I asked, puzzled. "Another souvenir?"

Both Holmes and Abberline looked at me, surprised by my suggestion. It was Lusk, however, who offered an explanation. "To wipe his hands, perhaps, Doctor. To clean the blood from his blade."

Holmes, lost in thought, stood up and walked towards me, his brow furrowed in concentration.

"Both murders, occurring on the same night," observed Abberline, rising to his feet, "seem to have been interrupted. Yet, there's no doubt they were committed by the same hand."

Holmes rejoined Lusk and me, his expression grim. "In Stride's case, the killer was thwarted before he could fully indulge his proclivities," he stated, his voice laced with a hint of frustration. He paused, then added, his eyes hardening, "But the urge, gentlemen, it would not have been sated. It would have lingered, festering, demanding release." I caught the subtle shift in his demeanour, the almost imperceptible hardening of his gaze, but the others seemed oblivious.

Holmes gestured towards the second victim, her mutilated form testament to the killer's depravity. "Fate, it seems, offered him a second chance, and he seized it with relish. Another unfortunate woman, lured into the shadows, where he could complete his gruesome ritual undisturbed."

As he spoke, a constable pushed his way through the crowd, his face etched with a mixture of apprehension and excitement. He hesitated, clearly wanting to address Abberline privately, but the presence of Holmes, Lusk, and myself seemed to give him pause.

"Out with it, lad," Abberline prompted, his voice sharp.

"Sir," the constable began, "several witnesses have identified the deceased as Catherine Eddowes, a woman of, and shall we say, ill repute, known to frequent this area. They claim to recognise her clothing."

"Catherine Eddowes," Abberline repeated, his brow furrowing in thought.

I glanced at Holmes, but he seemed lost in his own world, his gaze fixed on the murdered woman, yet seeing something far beyond the grim reality before us. A flicker of anger, of cold fury, burned in his eyes. The sheer audacity of the killer, claiming two victims in a single night, was a blatant disregard for the combined efforts of Scotland Yard, of Holmes himself, and of the entire Metropolitan Police force.

It was Holmes' uncharacteristic silence, the stillness of his normally restless form that spoke volumes. I had never seen him so utterly defeated.

The pieces of the puzzle began to fall into place. Elizabeth Stride, murdered roughly an hour before Catherine Eddowes, had been spared the full extent of the killer's savagery. Eddowes, however, had borne the brunt of his frustrated rage.

"Stride's face was untouched," observed Lusk, his voice thoughtful, "but Eddowes' is mutilated. Perhaps she knew her killer. Perhaps she could identify him."

It was a shrewd observation, and both Holmes and Abberline exchanged glances, considering its implications. Meanwhile, the crowd continued to swell, their morbid curiosity drawing them ever closer to the gruesome spectacle.

A sense of unease settled over me. It seemed unwise to linger at close proximity to the growing throng. The air crackled with tension, the whispers and murmurs of the crowd growing louder, more agitated. I recalled the recent clashes between the police and unemployed workers, the so-called "Bloody Sunday" that had left thirteen dead and many more injured. Public sentiment was already volatile, and these latest murders threatened to ignite a powder keg of unrest. The risk of another riot, fueled by fear and frustration, seemed all too real.

Sensing the shift in the crowd's mood, Abberline made a swift decision. "The bodies must be removed to the mortuary at once," he declared. "Gentlemen, I suggest we adjourn to a more private location to discuss this matter further."

Lusk, ever the pragmatist, offered the use of the Crown Club on Mile End Road, a welcome alternative to the stuffy confines of the Commercial Street police station. We agreed, and soon our carriage was once again threading its way through the crowded streets.

"Holmes," Lusk began, breaking the silence that had settled over us, "what do you make of this dreadful business?"

Holmes' response was immediate, almost theatrical, suggesting he'd been anticipating the question, his answer already formulated in his mind. He rose from his seat at the Crown Club, pacing back and forth as he spoke, his voice taking on a dramatic cadence. He was so animated, so utterly engrossed in his reconstruction of the events, that I felt transported back to Burner Street, as if witnessing the murders unfold before my very eyes. He strode across the room, his movements mirroring, I imagined, the killer's path, the geography of the crime scene imprinted on his mind.

"The moment I arrived, gentlemen," he declared, striking a pose that wouldn't have been out of place on a stage, "one crucial detail became abundantly clear."

"Stride was murdered directly in front of the International Working Men's Educational Club. Directly in front, you see." He pointed towards an imaginary doorway, his voice ringing with conviction. "Burner Street." The scene, as he described it, sprang to life in my mind's eye.

"What this tells us is, gentlemen, that our killer is intimately familiar with this area. These murders, each one seemingly opportunistic, suggest a man who operates within a limited geographical radius. He either lives in Whitechapel, or he frequents it regularly."

Abberline and Lusk listened intently, captivated by Holmes' dramatic pronouncements. Both men, it was clear, were desperate for a solution, for an end to the reign of terror that gripped their community.

"I made inquiries about the meeting held at the club last night," Holmes continued, his voice regaining its normal cadence. "A discussion, it seems, on socialism and Semitism. I overheard a constable mention that the talk touched upon issues of housing and unemployment – topics that tend to stir the passions of the more leftist elements of society." It was clear that even while examining the bodies, Holmes had remained attuned to the conversations swirling around him.

"The atmosphere, I gather, was rather heated," he added. "This area, as you know, is not particularly tolerant of differing viewpoints. A volatile mix, gentlemen, a volatile mix indeed." Abberline nodded grimly, confirming Holmes' assessment.

"If our killer attended this meeting," Holmes mused, his voice taking on a speculative tone, "he would have emerged in a highly agitated state. And what better way to release that pent-up frustration than to unleash it upon an unsuspecting victim?" He paused, then, with a sudden, startling transformation, he became the killer.

It was a remarkable performance, worthy of the finest stage actor. His posture shifted, his eyes hardened, his voice deepening as he stalked across the room, embodying the killer's rage and frustration.

"He leaves the meeting, seething with resentment," Holmes growled, his voice dripping with venom. "'This society,' he mutters, 'this damned society, it casts me out, treats me like dirt!'" The words, delivered with chilling conviction, sent a shiver down my spine. He continued his imaginary journey, his steps heavy with anger. Then, spotting his imaginary victim, he lunged, his hands outstretched, his face contorted in a mask of fury.

27.

A moment later, the transformation was complete. Holmes, the actor, vanished, replaced by Holmes, the detective, his gaze sharp and analytical. The image of the simulated murder, however, lingered in my mind, a chilling reminder of the darkness that lurked in the heart of Whitechapel.

"The second murder, gentlemen," Holmes began, his voice regaining its usual crispness, "offers more insights into the killer's profile." Abberline leaned forward, his expression intent. While Lusk and I had been captivated by Holmes' dramatic reconstruction, Abberline, the pragmatic policeman, was focused on the facts, the tangible clues that might lead to the killer's capture. Holmes, it seemed, was illuminating the shadows, revealing details that had eluded even the keenest minds at Scotland Yard.

"Catherine Eddowes, as you know, was murdered in Mitre Square," Holmes continued. "A quarter to two in the morning. Constable Edward Watkins discovered the body some ten minutes later." Abberline nodded, confirming the details.

"Twelve minutes, gentlemen," added Holmes, "that's all it takes to walk from Burner Street to Mitre Square. I timed it myself on our way here." Lusk nodded knowingly, his intimate familiarity with the streets of Whitechapel proving invaluable.

"Even after the passage of time," Holmes continued, "a thorough examination of the crime scene can yield valuable insights. It allows us to, as it were, step into the killer's shoes, to understand his thought processes, his motivations."

"One must learn to think like a criminal, to see the world through their eyes." He paused, then, with a dramatic flourish, he transported us back to Mitre Square, his words painting a vivid picture of the scene. He pointed towards an imaginary lane, his voice taking on a hushed, almost conspiratorial tone.

"This side of the square, gentlemen, opens onto a narrow passage. From this vantage point, one has a clear view of anyone approaching. A policeman on patrol, for instance, would be visible long before he reached the square."

He then proceeded to describe the surroundings in meticulous detail, as if Eddowes's body still lay before him.

"The Eddowes murder, gentlemen, is particularly brutal," Holmes stated, his voice grim. "The throat slashed, the abdomen eviscerated, and, most disturbingly, the face mutilated."

Abberline was quick to offer his opinion, "I believe it was the culmination of his pent-up rage, the frustration of being interrupted during the Stride murder."

"Perhaps," added Lusk, "He disfigured her, Holmes, because she recognized him. It's the only explanation."

Holmes, however, shook his head, dismissing their suggestions. "I believe that, gentlemen, the truth lies elsewhere." He gestured towards the imaginary body. "Picture the scene. Our killer, thwarted in his previous attempt, is consumed by a furious need for release. When I arrived at Mitre Square, a different scenario began to unfold in my mind. I shall endeavour to illustrate it for you. Allow the images I conjure to take hold."

We fell silent, our attention riveted on Holmes.

He beckoned me forward. "Watson, if you please." I joined him, feeling as though I were under a hypnotic spell. He positioned me on a specific spot, then took up a position behind me.

Suddenly, Holmes reached out with his left hand, as if to touch my face. Instinctively, I recoiled.

"Our killer approaches his victim from behind," Holmes explained, his voice low and intense. "He attempts to slash her throat, but she reacts, just as you did, Watson. He's off balance, his position compromised. So, he spins her around, forcing her against the wall." He gestured towards my left, indicating the location of the imaginary wall. "This way, the blood splatter is directed away from him."

"But now," he continued, his grip tightening around my shoulders, "her throat is not so easily accessible." He began to mime strangling me, his actions becoming increasingly realistic. I squirmed, uncomfortable with the intensity of his performance, but he seemed oblivious, caught up in his reconstruction of the crime. I could see Lusk and Abberline watching us, their faces a mixture of fascination and apprehension.

"He uses his left arm to constrict her airway," Holmes narrated, his grip tightening. "Normally, unconsciousness would follow swiftly, but she struggles, just as you are doing now, Watson."

He grabbed my hair, yanking my head back, and mimed drawing a blade across my throat with his right hand. My struggles only served to make his movements more erratic, his hand passing across my face several times. Finally, with a dramatic flourish, he released his grip, his imaginary blade completing its gruesome task.

I collapsed onto the floor, rubbing my neck gingerly, half-convinced that I'd actually been injured. I glanced up at Lusk and Abberline, their faces pale and shocked. Holmes, still caught up in his performance, pointed towards me, his voice ringing with dramatic intensity.

"He attempts to restrain her head with his left hand, while his right wields the blade," Holmes explained, his voice still laced with the killer's intensity. "But she resists, struggles fiercely. His first few attempts go awry, the blade slicing across her face, not her throat." He mimed the frantic movements, his hand passing over my imaginary face. "Finally, he manages to overpower her, and she falls still. Only then, as he turns her towards him, does he see the damage he's inflicted." He gently turned my imaginary body towards him, his voice softening slightly.

It was a chillingly effective demonstration. Without Holmes' dramatic enactment, the sequence of events, the chaotic struggle, would have remained unclear.

"The mutilation of her face, gentlemen," Holmes continued, his voice returning to its normal cadence, "was not premeditated. It was a consequence of the victim's resistance, an unintended, though not unwelcome, result." He gestured towards my position on the floor. "He didn't plan to disfigure her, but nor did he regret it."

Holmes offered me his hand, and I pulled myself up, still slightly shaken by the intensity of his performance. As I made my way back to my chair, Holmes knelt down, examining the spot where I had lain.

To my relief, Holmes continued his demonstration without further involving me. He knelt over the imaginary body, his movements taking on a frantic, almost frenzied quality as he mimed the act of evisceration. We watched, transfixed, as he meticulously reenacted the gruesome ritual of the Whitechapel murderer.

"Even in death," Holmes narrated, his voice taking on a chillingly detached tone, "Catherine Eddowes was not spared. Jack, as he now styles himself, was not yet satisfied. He proceeded to open her abdomen, to remove, to 'Rip'..." He paused, his hand plunging into the imaginary cavity. "This."

He withdrew his hand, holding aloft an imaginary organ. He didn't need to name it. We all knew what it was – the womb, the killer's macabre trophy.

"Recall, gentlemen," Holmes continued, his voice returning to its normal cadence, "the missing piece of Eddowes's apron. Lusk correctly surmised that it was used to wipe the killer's hands." He mimed the act of cleaning his hands on the imaginary cloth, his movements so vivid, so realistic, that I felt a prickle of fear at the back of my neck. He was there, in that moment, reliving the killer's actions, seeing the world through his eyes. It was a chillingly effective performance, and I could see both Lusk and Abberline struggling to maintain their composure.

He mimed wiping his hands on the imaginary apron piece, then stood up, the imaginary womb still clutched in his hand, his face contorted in a mask of triumph. It was as if we had been transported back to Mitre Square, witnessing the gruesome spectacle firsthand. I could almost see the glint of blood in the moonlight, reflecting in the killer's eyes.

"He took the wombs of Nichols and Chapman," Holmes stated, his voice returning to its normal cadence, stepping out of character and addressing us directly. "He would have taken Stride's as well, had he not been interrupted. He craves them, gentlemen. With Eddowes, he finally sated his gruesome appetite."

A heavy silence fell over the room, the weight of his words pressing down on us.

"By the time the police arrived," Holmes continued, his voice low and grim, "Jack had vanished into the shadows."

The spell was broken. The vivid images conjured by Holmes' performance began to fade, replaced by the stark reality of the room around us. Holmes, his role as storyteller complete, returned to his seat, his demeanour calm and collected, as if he hadn't just led us on a chilling journey into the heart of darkness.

28.

Lusk, ever the gracious host, had arranged for lunch to be served, and we ate in near silence, the gruesome details of the morning's discoveries hanging heavy in the air.

Once the meal was concluded, Lusk, after a moment of quiet contemplation, spoke. "This demonstrates, gentlemen, that despite our best efforts, despite the increased police presence, this fiend operates with impunity, seemingly unconcerned about capture." He paused, his gaze hardening. "But capture him we must. It is our duty, our moral imperative." He continued, his voice taking on a more analytical tone. "He barely escaped detection at Burner Street. And at Mitre Square, according to Holmes, he practically strolled past a constable. Yet, his surgical skills are undeniable. This, at least, narrows the field of suspects."

Lusk turned to me, his expression thoughtful. "Doctor," he began, "as a man of medicine, you must have some insight into this...surgical precision."

I understood his meaning. He wasn't accusing me, but seeking my professional opinion. "Even a skilled surgeon," I replied, "would find such procedures challenging in the darkness. And even under ideal conditions, such an operation would require a minimum of thirty minutes." I paused, feeling a surge of professional pride. "Furthermore, I assure you, Mr. Lusk that a true physician would use their skills to heal, not to harm. To save lives, not to take them." My words, perhaps, were a touch more forceful than intended, fueled by a desire to defend the honour of my profession.

"Dr. Phillips, who examined Annie Chapman's body, stated that such precision could be achieved by perhaps one in a thousand," Lusk added, his tone not accusatory, but simply stating a fact. "And as we've seen, one of the two victims discovered this morning bears similar wounds." I conceded his point, remaining silent.

I noticed, however, that Holmes's gaze was fixed intently upon Abberline. Lusk, following my line of sight, seemed to notice as well. Abberline, since lunch, had been unusually quiet, lost in his own thoughts.

It became clear that Holmes was waiting for Abberline to speak, to make the next move in this silent game of cat and mouse. Lusk and I watched, like spectators at a chess match, anticipating the next strategic play. Holmes's unwavering gaze seemed to challenge Abberline, silently urging him to reveal his hand.

Finally, Abberline sighed, a deep, weary sound. He raised his head slowly, his gaze sweeping across our faces before settling on Holmes. He nodded slowly, a flicker of understanding in his eyes.

I was completely lost. Lusk and I exchanged puzzled glances.

"I made a mistake, gentlemen," Abberline admitted, his voice heavy with self-reproach. "A grave mistake. I believed, nay, I was certain that our killer was left-handed. I even released several suspects based on that assumption. The postmortem reports, from Doctors Llewellyn and Phillips, seemed to confirm it. But..." He paused, swallowing hard, his throat suddenly dry. "Based on Holmes's reconstruction of the Eddowes murder, it seems our man is right-handed."

"Never be afraid to question your assumptions, Abberline," Holmes said, his tone gentle, yet his words seemed only to deepen Abberline's sense of guilt. A sharp reprimand might have been easier to bear than Holmes's quiet understanding.

"Gentlemen," Abberline began, his gaze fixed on the table before him, "there is a matter... a sensitive matter, which I feel compelled to share with you. A piece of information that has been withheld from the public, kept secret by the police."

Holmes and I exchanged glances, surprised by this unexpected revelation.

"What's this, Abberline?" Lusk demanded, his voice rising in anger. "Information kept from the public? What sort of game are you playing?"

"I must ask for your absolute discretion in this matter," Abberline pleaded, his gaze sweeping across our faces. "You must promise me, gentlemen, that what I am about to reveal will not be made public. I trust you... but I need your word."

We remained silent, our curiosity piqued, but also wary of the implications of such a promise.

Abberline sighed, a deep, weary sound, and rose from his chair. "Mr. Lusk," he instructed, "have your most trusted driver bring your carriage around. There's something I need to show you, something that must remain strictly confidential."

Intrigued, we rose to our feet.

"Gulston Street, gentlemen," Abberline announced, his voice low and serious. "That is where we must go."

29.

Gulston Street was deserted, eerily quiet. Abberline directed our driver to a specific location, then instructed us to remain inside the carriage.

"Best we observe from here, gentlemen," he explained, gesturing towards a section of wall visible through the left-hand window. "Less chance of attracting unwanted attention."

We peered out, eager to see what Abberline deemed so important, but I, for one, saw nothing out of the ordinary. Just a plain brick wall. Lusk, judging by his perplexed expression, was equally baffled.

Holmes, however, after a moment's scrutiny, turned to Abberline, his eyes gleaming with a sudden intensity. "Something has been erased from that wall, hasn't it, Inspector?"

"Around three in the morning," Abberline explained, "amidst all the chaos, someone scrawled a message on this wall. It's less than five hundred metres from where Eddowes was murdered. Our officers, thinking it anti-Semitic, erased it."

I was about to question its relevance when Abberline continued. "Holmes has consistently highlighted certain observations, and my instincts told me you should know. Commissioner Warren, upon seeing it around four a.m., ordered its removal to prevent potential riots."

Silence settled over us.

Lusk cleared his throat. "This area is home to many migrants, mostly Jews. They're not well-liked by some. If word spreads that the killer might be Jewish, we could face riots."

"What did it say?" Holmes asked calmly. Vandalism wasn't unusual, so I wondered why Abberline deemed it significant.

Abberline hesitated, choosing his words carefully. "The Commissioner himself ordered its removal. In fact, he was already on the scene when I arrived."

"What?" Holmes, usually so composed, straightened abruptly. "He was there before you even saw it?"

Before anyone could respond, Holmes exited the carriage and strode towards the wall. We followed, our curiosity piqued. He stood before the scrubbed brick, his hand raised as if to write, but I realised he was gauging the height of the vandal.

"Five foot three, perhaps five foot six," he declared, turning to us, confirming my suspicion.

We gathered at the wall, examining the faint remnants of the erased message. The white chalk on red brick had been thoroughly scrubbed, making it nearly impossible to decipher.

Holmes traced the ghostly outlines with his fingers, peering through his magnifying glass, his keen eyes searching for any lingering clues. "This, gentlemen," he declared, his voice laced with frustration, "could have been a valuable piece of the puzzle. If only we knew what it said."

"Mr. Lusk," Holmes said, turning to the gentleman, "would you be so kind as to dispatch your driver for a bottle of vinegar? With all haste, if you please." The driver, overhearing the request, looked down at us expectantly.

Lusk nodded, and the carriage rattled off down the street.

The four of us stood before the wall, straining our eyes to decipher the ghostly traces of the erased message. Within minutes, Lusk's driver returned, bottle in hand. He passed it to Lusk, who, in turn, handed it to Holmes.

"Gentlemen," Holmes instructed, "if you would kindly step back." We obeyed, unsure of his intentions.

The driver, perched atop the carriage, watched with interest, his presence providing a convenient screen from any curious passersby.

Holmes uncorked the bottle and began to carefully splash the vinegar onto the section of wall where the message had been scrubbed away.

As if by magic, the faint, ghostly letters began to reappear, the acid in the vinegar reacting with the remnants of the chalk. A collective gasp escaped our lips. For a moment, I, too, was convinced that Holmes possessed supernatural powers.

The acidic vinegar reacted with the alkaline chalk, causing a faint effervescence and leaving a whiter residue where the message had been scrawled. The words, stark and undeniable, emerged from the brick like a ghostly apparition:

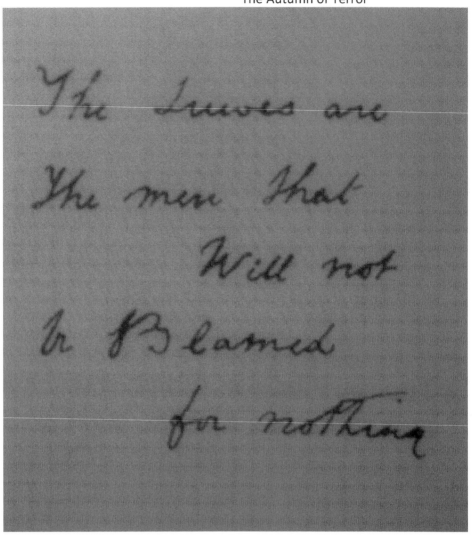

The Juews are

The men that

Will not be

Blamed for Nothing

"The Jews will not be blamed for anything," I murmured, reading the words aloud.

We stared at the message, its significance slowly dawning on us. The words, written in a flowing cursive script, were broken into five uneven lines. The misspelling of "Jews" as "Juews" hinted at the writer's lack of formal education.

"I still can't fathom why Warren ordered the message erased so quickly," Abberline mused, turning to Holmes for an explanation.

Holmes, however, seemed preoccupied. He was bent over, examining something on the ground near the wall, something we couldn't quite make out from our vantage point.

"The cursive script, the five uneven lines, the misspelling, all point to a writer of limited education," Holmes remarked, his voice detached, his attention still focused on the object in his hand.

We reread the message, the glaring error in the first word now even more apparent. "Juews," I murmured, shaking my head.

Holmes continued to scrutinise the object he'd found, turning it over and over in his hands. We, however, remained fixated on the message, trying to decipher its meaning, its purpose. It was as if Holmes, having performed his magic trick, had lost interest in the illusion itself, his mind already focused on a new, more intriguing puzzle.

He began to pace back and forth along the pavement, his eyes scanning the ground, as if searching for something lost. As he passed Abberline, he stopped, his gaze intense.

"You have those letters with you, I presume," Holmes said, his voice quiet, "the ones the newspapers received, supposedly from the killer?"

Abberline's eyes widened in understanding. He reached into his coat pocket, retrieving a handful of letters, and began to compare their script to the writing on the wall. A faint blush crept up his neck, a sign, I suspected, of embarrassment at not having made the connection himself. His thick sideburns, however, likely concealed it from Lusk and the driver.

Lusk and I peered over Abberline's shoulder, eager to see the results of his comparison.

"Well?" I prompted. "Is it a match?"

Abberline, his jaw clenched, let out a frustrated growl. "If that blithering idiot Warren hadn't ordered this scrubbed away, this would have been a much simpler task!" He shoved the letters back into his pocket, his face a mask of annoyance.

While Holmes's ingenuity had revealed the message, the vinegar wash had rendered the script too faint for a detailed comparison. Simply being able to read the words was a stroke of luck. Without Holmes's quick thinking, the message would have remained lost forever.

This incident, I suspected, would serve as a constant reminder to Abberline of the police's shortcomings, a humbling experience he was unlikely to forget, especially in Lusk's presence.

With a sigh of resignation, Abberline pulled out a notebook and pen, and began to meticulously copy the message from the wall, preserving what remained of this crucial piece of evidence.

Holmes rejoined us, his gaze fixed on Abberline, his expression serious. "This isn't an anti-Semitic message, Abberline," he stated. "It's a declaration. A proclamation, if you will."

Lusk frowned, clearly puzzled. "But if he were Jewish, why draw attention to it?"

"Perhaps," I ventured, "it was written by someone else, someone trying to implicate the Jewish community."

Abberline looked at me, a flicker of appreciation in his eyes. "It's a crime to tamper with evidence..." he began, but Holmes cut him short.

"And not the first time it's happened in this investigation," he added, his voice laced with barely suppressed anger. His ire, it seemed, was directed not just at Warren, but at the entire Whitechapel constabulary.

Abberline, however, seemed unfazed by the interruption. "The Commissioner believed it irrelevant, a mere act of vandalism intended to incite racial hatred. He ordered it erased to prevent further unrest."

Holmes, his gaze unwavering, fixed Abberline with a penetrating stare. "It's highly relevant, Abberline. Because it was written by the killer himself."

"What?!" Lusk exclaimed, his face paling.

"Precisely," Holmes affirmed, his voice ringing with conviction. "This, gentlemen, is the handiwork of the Whitechapel murderer."

30.

"This was erased to prevent racial tensions," Abberline murmured, still processing Holmes's revelation. But then his gaze followed Holmes's pointing finger to a piece of cloth on the ground nearby. His expression shifted immediately.

We all turned our attention to the fabric lying a few feet from the wall. My heart skipped a beat—I recognised it instantly. Abberline crouched down, picked up the cloth, and unfolded it. The torn edge confirmed my suspicion.

It was unmistakably a piece of Catherine Eddowes's apron.

"The shape of the tear, the colour, the pattern," Holmes stated, his voice calm and precise, "all correspond perfectly with the missing piece from Catherine Eddowes's apron."

Lusk's eyebrows shot up. He stepped closer to Abberline, examining the cloth with a newfound intensity.

Abberline, his face grim, nodded silently. The dark stains on the fabric were unmistakable – blood, wiped from the killer's hands.

Holmes, showing no sign of squeamishness, took the cloth from Abberline. He turned to us, his gaze holding ours.

"This, gentlemen, is why I believe the message on the wall was written by the murderer himself. The torn piece of apron, discarded beneath the message, is the link. He ripped it from her apron after the murder, used it to wipe his hands clean, and then discarded it here. Seeing the wall, he felt compelled to leave his mark, using the chalk he carried in his pocket." He paused, his eyes gleaming with a sudden intensity. "A man who carries chalk, gentlemen. Think about that. He was agitated, his mind racing. The flowing cursive script, the uneven lines – they speak of a mind in turmoil, pouring its rage onto the wall. He's saying, in essence, 'Now you have a real reason to blame the Jews, not just empty prejudice.'"

"You're suggesting..." Lusk began, his voice barely a whisper.

Holmes turned to him, his expression unwavering. "Yes, Mr. Lusk. I believe our killer is a Jew."

31.

At Lusk's behest, an urgent meeting of the Whitechapel Vigilance Committee was convened. Within the hour, the members, summoned by special messenger, began to arrive at the Crown Club. Holmes, Abberline, and I were granted permission to attend as Lusk's guests.

The atmosphere in the room was markedly different from the fear and agitation that gripped the streets outside. These men, the pillars of the Whitechapel community, maintained a veneer of calm, of composure, that I found both reassuring and slightly unsettling.

Their detachment from the raw emotion that permeated the East End seemed almost unnatural.

I had anticipated accusations, recriminations, perhaps even open hostility towards Abberline and the police in the wake of the double murder. Instead, the committee members, impeccably dressed and composed, took their seats around a large table, their demeanour that of businessmen conducting a routine meeting.

"Gentlemen," Lusk began, his voice calm and measured, "I am grateful to Inspector Abberline, who is leading the hunt for this bloodthirsty fiend, for setting aside our previous differences and joining us today. However, I must express our collective dissatisfaction with the progress of this investigation. You all know Mr. Frederick Abberline. Our committee has pledged its full support to his efforts. However, given the ineffectiveness of the local constabulary, we have seen fit to engage the services of private detectives." He paused, his gaze sweeping across the assembled faces. "Given the gravity of the situation, I trust you will not object to this decision. The situation is deteriorating rapidly, and we must avail ourselves of every possible resource."

A heavy silence descended upon the room.

Lusk turned to us, his expression serious. "That being said, I prefer that the identities of these detectives remain confidential. Therefore, I shall introduce them to you using a code familiar to our fraternity." He paused for dramatic effect. "Gentlemen, meet Messrs. J and H Bachelor, the two individuals I have personally engaged to solve these crimes. I had also extended an invitation to Mr. Le Grand, but he expressed his regrets, citing business that needed to be attended to." He continued, his voice taking on a more optimistic tone. "These gentlemen have uncovered some promising leads, though they have not yet succeeded in apprehending the culprit."

"What news of the investigation?" a voice called out from the assembled members. I couldn't place the speaker, but the question hung heavy in the air, charged with an unspoken accusation.

I felt as though we were on trial, facing a jury of stern and unforgiving judges. The atmosphere in the room had shifted, a palpable tension replacing the earlier composure. I glanced at Holmes and Abberline, and saw a similar unease reflected in their faces. Their shared discomfort, however, offered me a strange sort of solace.

"Mr. H. Bachelor," Lusk announced, his voice carrying across the room, "believes the killer to be a Jew. Perhaps he can elaborate on his reasoning." Lusk, who had been standing, now took his seat, his gaze fixed on Holmes. Abberline and I exchanged glances. The Crown Club, so recently a place of convivial lunching, had transformed into a courtroom, the air thick with anticipation.

Holmes rose to his feet, his demeanour calm and collected. All eyes turned towards him.

"Gentlemen," he began, his voice clear and steady, "let me preface my remarks by stating unequivocally that my deductions in no way imply a condemnation of the entire Jewish community. I trust you will not interpret my words as anti-Semitic." I breathed a sigh of relief. Holmes, in his usual blunt and forthright manner, could sometimes be undiplomatic. This gathering, however, demanded a more nuanced approach.

"There are murderers in every community," Holmes began, his voice steady. "What I'm asserting is that the evidence points to our suspect, 'Jack the Ripper,' being of Jewish descent."

"Could it not be," interjected a gentleman beside Lusk, his tone calm yet probing, "that an anti-Semite committed these acts, intending to frame a Jew?"

"If that were the case," Holmes replied, "we'd be dealing with a meticulous planner, not an impulsive killer. The handwriting lacks the precision of premeditation. Its fluidity suggests it was penned in a moment of fervour. Serial killers like this one feel neither regret nor guilt. This writing reflects that intensity—a hallmark of a disturbed mind."

The room remained silent, the air thick with anticipation, as if awaiting further elucidation from Holmes.

"The message on the wall suggests our man was deeply affected by the discussion held last night at the club near where Stride was murdered," Holmes continued, his voice taking on a more analytical tone. "He was likely incensed by the perceived social injustices discussed. Stride was killed, gentlemen, directly in front of that club. And the meeting, I understand, was attended primarily by Jews. Whatever was discussed there clearly resonated with 'Jack.' It was this agitation, this pent-up rage that fueled the attack on Stride. Thwarted in his initial attempt, he then turned his fury upon Eddowes. Yet, even after these brutal acts, his anger remained. The message on the wall is a testament to that lingering resentment."

I saw several committee members nod in agreement.

Holmes continued, his gaze sweeping across the room, ensuring he held the attention of every man present. "He wanted to express his outrage, to make a statement. He felt unjustly accused, persecuted simply for being Jewish. A target of suspicion, an outcast from respectable society. He was treated unfairly, gentlemen, judged without cause. And so, in a fit of rage, he commits these horrific acts, then leaves this defiant message on the wall. 'Now,' he's saying, 'you have a reason to blame me. Now I've earned your scorn.'"

Holmes turned to Abberline, his gaze intense, as if seeking confirmation of his theory. Abberline remained silent, but a deep frown creased his brow.

"Note the spelling and grammatical errors," Holmes continued, his voice sharp and precise. "They speak of a limited education. But more than that, gentlemen, they suggest a mind in decline, ravaged by the insidious effects of syphilis. I believe our killer is deteriorating, both mentally and physically. He cannot maintain this gruesome charade much longer. This message, this desperate cry for recognition, is the product of a mind consumed by rage and clouded by disease." He looked from Lusk to Abberline, his gaze unwavering. "That is my conclusion."

He paused, then added, "The proximity of Stride's murder to the Jewish socialist meeting, and the discovery of the apron piece near this message, offer another crucial insight."

"And what is that, Mr. Holmes?" Abberline asked, his voice sharp with anticipation.

"It tells us, gentlemen," Holmes declared, his voice rising with each word, "that our killer is a Jewish businessman. A Jew. A businessman. And he is here, in this very room!"

"How dare you, sir!" a voice roared from the assembled men. A figure rose abruptly from his chair, his face flushed with anger, shattering the veneer of composure that had held the meeting in its grip.

A flicker of triumph crossed Holmes's lips, which he quickly suppressed. I breathed a sigh of relief. I had watched with growing unease, fearing that Holmes's pronouncements might spark another social conflagration. London, already on edge, could not afford further unrest. Abberline, too, seemed apprehensive, his gaze darting nervously towards Holmes as he spoke, clearly aware of the potential consequences of his words.

The gentleman who had risen to his feet remained standing, his face contorted with rage, his body trembling with barely controlled fury.

Holmes, however, seemed unfazed. He returned to his seat, his demeanour calm and collected. He paused for a moment, letting the silence hang heavy in the air, before continuing, his voice now quiet and measured.

"This man's religion, gentlemen," he began, his gaze sweeping across the room, "is irrelevant to his crimes. Murderers come from all walks of life, all faiths. African, European, Asian, it matters not. They are driven by something deeper, something darker, than mere religious or racial affiliation. They suffer from psychological afflictions that transcend such superficial distinctions. They belong, not to a particular race or creed, but to a different category altogether – the category of the psychologically disturbed. That being said," He added, his voice hardening slightly, "I stand by my assertion. Jack the Ripper is a Jew."

The enraged gentleman slowly sank back into his chair, his anger seemingly deflated by Holmes's unexpected shift in tone.

"His Jewishness, however," Holmes continued, turning to Lusk, "is incidental to his being Jack the Ripper. He is simply a man, afflicted by a disease that is slowly destroying his mind." He paused, letting the weight of his words sink in, reiterating his conclusion, in a voice calm and collected.

32.

Holmes, Abberline, and I excused ourselves from the Vigilance Committee meeting, sensing that the discussions would continue late into the night. At the time of our departure, the committee was drafting a letter to Lord Salisbury's government, proposing a substantial reward for information leading to the apprehension of "Jack the Ripper." They believed such an incentive might persuade those with knowledge of the crimes to come forward, breaking the wall of silence that shielded the killer.

Lusk provided us with transport back to Baker Street. His trusted driver, following his employer's instructions, first dropped Abberline at the Whitechapel police station before continuing on to our destination.

As we drove through the darkened streets of Whitechapel, Abberline leaned closer, his voice dropping to a hushed whisper, as if unwilling to be overheard, even by the driver perched above. His caution spoke volumes about the level of distrust that permeated the investigation.

"Were it not for the testimony of those two coachmen," he murmured, referring to the drivers who had corroborated Holmes's account of the previous night's events, "your friend would still be languishing in a cell." His words, surprisingly, were filled with gratitude towards the men, a stark contrast to the animosity I'd expected.

Despite the quasi-judicial atmosphere of the meeting, Abberline, like Holmes and myself, had sensed a genuine concern for the community amongst the assembled businessmen. Their motives, it seemed, were pure, their desire to see justice served, untainted by personal agendas.

Abberline's attempts at conversation, I realised, were an effort to break the oppressive silence that had settled over us. His destination, thankfully, was not far off.

"I knew you were conducting inquiries in the area incognito, Holmes," Abberline admitted, his voice barely audible above the rumble of the carriage wheels, "but I confess, I hadn't pictured you to do so, disguised as a woman."

"Only Lusk and those two coachmen were privy to my disguise, Abberline," Holmes replied, a hint of amusement in his voice. "Even my esteemed colleague here was kept in the dark. Not out of any lack of trust, Watson, I assure you, but simply because I preferred to keep my cards close to my chest in this particular game. I trust you understand."

"Indeed, Holmes, a sound strategy," Abberline conceded. "I've decided to employ a similar tactic myself. Two of my most trusted men will be patrolling the area in disguise, starting tomorrow. An excellent approach, though I must point out, Watson, that your friend made a rather elementary error."

"We'll ensure your men are better briefed, Abberline," Holmes chuckled. "Instruct your constables to employ a simple challenge-and-response system. 'Are you one of us?' should suffice. I wager that with a few strategically placed officers, disguised as women, we could not only apprehend this Ripper fellow, but also significantly reduce street crime across London."

"Fortunately, Holmes," Abberline replied dryly, "the entirety of London does not fall under my jurisdiction. I shall be content to restore order to H Division." H Division, of course, encompassed Whitechapel, and Abberline, in the wake of the murders, had been given carte blanche to oversee all criminal investigations within its boundaries.

"Abberline," Holmes said, his brow furrowed, his gaze encompassing both the Inspector and myself, "this information must remain strictly confidential. I suspect, as you may have surmised, that Lusk is receiving advice from another source. And judging by his recent actions, that advice mirrors my own." He paused, his eyes questioning.

"Lusk did mention engaging two private detectives," Abberline confirmed, "due to the perceived incompetence of the local police. I assumed he meant you and Watson."

"He introduced us as 'Messrs. J and H Bachelor'," Holmes pointed out. "John and Holmes, both unmarried. A rather transparent code, wouldn't you say?"

"He also mentioned a certain 'Le Grand'," Holmes recalled.

"Presumably another code name," I mused.

Abberline rolled his eyes. "The last thing we can be assured of, gentlemen, is anonymity. Thanks to a certain monthly column in The Strand, our exploits are hardly a secret." He smiled, and Holmes's lips twitched in response.

"The question is," Holmes said, his voice taking on a more serious tone, "who is this Le Grand?"

"'Le Grand'," I mused aloud, "it's French, isn't it? Meaning 'the great,' or 'the large.' Perhaps it refers to someone of considerable stature, an expert in their field." I knew, of course, that both Holmes and Abberline were perfectly familiar with the French language. My stating the obvious, a habit Holmes often chided me for, seemed particularly pointless in this instance.

Yet, my seemingly innocuous comment seemed to spark a connection in their minds. They exchanged glances, a silent understanding passing between them.

"Don't misunderstand me, Holmes," Abberline said, his voice taking on a more conciliatory tone. "I still have reservations about Lusk involving outsiders in this investigation. Not everyone possesses your unique qualifications. However," he added, his expression grim, "in this instance, I'm willing to accept any assistance that might bring an end to these atrocities." His words surprised both Holmes and myself. Abberline, it seemed, was willing to set aside his professional pride in the face of this unprecedented crisis.

Holmes sank back into his seat, a shadow of frustration crossing his face. "So close," he murmured, his voice laced with disappointment. "We almost had him."

"Rest assured, Holmes," Abberline replied, his tone reassuring, "this incident will remain confidential. My respect for your methods compels me to discretion." He was referring, of course, to Holmes's ill-fated foray into undercover work. "Your strategy was sound, Holmes. We were on the verge of a breakthrough. A damned shame, it is. A damned shame." Abberline's words, though supportive, couldn't mask the underlying tension. Holmes's frustration was palpable, his silence more eloquent than any outburst. I sensed a storm brewing beneath his calm exterior, something he was holding back. Something he wasn't yet ready to share.

I made a mental note to inquire later, but before I could formulate a question, Abberline leaned closer, his voice dropping to a conspiratorial whisper.

"Holmes," he murmured, "be warned. There are forces at work within the constabulary itself, forces that seek to undermine my investigation. They orchestrated your arrest, Holmes, to discredit you, to make a mockery of your methods." He turned to me, his voice even lower.

"That Reid fellow, he's a venomous snake. He was determined to see Holmes hauled before a magistrate. A blatant abuse of power. Lusk's complaints about the police, about their incompetence and corruption, I'm beginning to think he was right all along. I suspected outside interference, but I never imagined the rot would run so deep."

We reached the Commercial Street police station, and Abberline prepared to disembark. My respect for the man had grown considerably. He was fighting a lonely battle against a formidable foe, not just the Whitechapel murderer, but the corruption within his own ranks. He was, at heart, a true detective, a man dedicated to justice. With a final, courteous tip of his hat, he stepped out of the carriage, turned, and disappeared into the night.

I watched Abberline stride towards the police station, my position in the carriage affording me a clear view. I had chosen this seat deliberately, hoping for a face-to-face conversation with Holmes on our return to Baker Street. As Abberline disappeared from sight, a commotion drew my attention—a constable running towards us, shouting something indistinct.

Our carriage halted abruptly.

"Mr. Reid said to take this with you," the constable called, tossing a bundle of cloth through the window before tapping the carriage twice, signaling the driver to continue. He then turned and walked back to the station.

Curious, I reached for the bundle, but Holmes intercepted it, casting it aside dismissively. "Don't trouble yourself," he muttered.

Any hope of engaging Holmes in conversation was dashed. He remained silent throughout the journey, gazing out of the window, as immobile as a Greek statue carved from marble.

I wasn't surprised that Holmes's disguise had attracted unwanted attention, nearly resulting in his arrest. It was a risk we both knew existed. Yet, the disdainful treatment he received from the constabulary stung deeply. Adding to the sense of unease was the revelation that Lusk and the Vigilance Committee had engaged another detective. Doubts about our capabilities gnawed at me, leaving a bitter taste of inadequacy.

Lost in these troubling thoughts, the journey back to Baker Street passed in a blur.

33.

The carriage pulled up outside 221B Baker Street, but before we could alight, a commotion erupted on the street, capturing our attention. Newspaper boys, their voices hoarse from shouting, darted through the throng, brandishing the latest edition. People were gathering eagerly to buy it.

"Double murder! Another double murder! Read all about it!" one of them cried, his words drawing me in like a moth to a flame. I pushed my way through the crowd, eager to get my hands on a copy. And when I saw the headline, my jaw dropped.

The words, printed in bold, stark type, sent a shiver down my spine: "JACK the RIPPER" MURDERS AGAIN. DOUBLE EVENT IN LONDON'S EAST END. Numerous suspects being questioned by Scotland Yard.

My hands trembled as I scanned the lurid details. The sheer horror of it all was overwhelming. I sank onto a nearby bench, my legs suddenly weak, the newspaper clutched in my hand.

Bodies of two women, one on Burner Street at St. George and the other in Mitre Square in Aldgate, were discovered early this morning. The brutal nature of the murders suggests they are yet more victims of Jack the Ripper.

I read the headline again, the words blurring before my eyes. The sheer horror of it, coupled with the exhaustion of the day, threatened to overwhelm me. I sat there on the cold stone bench, momentarily forgetting my purpose, the newspaper clutched in my trembling hand. It was only then that I realised Holmes was nowhere to be seen. Folding the paper, I tucked it into my pocket and made my way back to Baker Street, a knot of anxiety tightening in my chest.

The ascent to our rooms at 221B felt unusually arduous, my legs heavy, and my mind weighed down by the grim events of the day. Halfway up the stairs, I encountered a telegraph boy, descending after delivering a message. Holmes, then, was already aware. I continued my climb, each step an effort of will.

Holmes was seated on the sofa when I entered, his gaze fixed on some distant point, his face pale and drawn. I silently proffered the newspaper.

"Do you recall, Watson," he murmured, his voice flat and devoid of emotion, "what I said when Lusk first consulted us? I told you then, we could not solve his problem."

He had, indeed. On any other day, I would have pressed him, demanded to know how he could have foreseen such a grim outcome. But my own spirits were too low, my mind too troubled, to pursue the matter. I placed the newspaper on the teapoy and sank into my chair.

Holmes seemed disinclined to discuss the events of the night, and I, sensing his need for respite, held my tongue. He needed time to process, to regroup.

"You romanticise these matters, Watson," he remarked, his voice tinged with a hint of irritation. I realised he'd been perusing my notebook, his keen eyes dissecting my account of the investigation, as he held it in his hands. He frowned, setting the book aside, and proceeded to fill his pipe from his Persian slipper.

"Deduction, observation, these are sciences, Watson, not fodder for your sensationalist prose. One must approach them with objectivity, with rigour, not with the fanciful flourishes of a romantic novelist. You cannot expect to apply the principles of Euclid to the vagaries of human emotion." He lit his pipe, leaning back against the cushions, the smoke curling upwards towards the gaslight.

"There are details, Watson, that are extraneous, irrelevant. One must focus on causality, on the essential elements of the case. You, however, seem determined to record every stray observation, as if quantity were a substitute for quality." He stretched out on the sofa, his eyes closed. "What, precisely, does the press have to say?"

His apparent calmness reassured me. He was, I knew, capable of absorbing the horrors I was about to relate. But there was something I needed to ask him first.

"I saw a messenger leave," I said, settling back into my chair.

"From Lusk," Holmes replied, his voice flat. "Seems his letter, addressed to Lord Salisbury, requesting for a government reward has been denied by Henry Matthews, the Home Secretary. The committee is now considering offering a private bounty."

I retrieved the newspaper from the teapoy and moved towards the window, perching on the sill. "Listen to this, Holmes," I began, reading aloud:

"'JACK the RIPPER" murders again. Double event in London's East end. Numerous suspects being questioned by Scotland Yard. Two More Victims Found in East London. Robbery does not appear to be a motive in either case, nor do the crimes bear the hallmarks of a common street brawl or assault. The bodies of two women were discovered early this morning, one in a passageway off Burner Street, near St. George's-in-the-East, the other in Mitre Square, Aldgate. The savage nature of the killings points, once again, to the fiendish hand of 'Jack the Ripper.' Whatever the circumstances, two more names have been added to the grim tally of victims, both, tragically, from the East End. A dark cloud hangs over this district, a sense of dread that a malevolent force stalks these streets, preying upon vulnerable women. These latest atrocities bear a chilling resemblance to the previous murders, suggesting a pattern, a ritualistic element, to the killer's methods.

Both crimes appear to have been premeditated, the locations chosen with care. The distance between the two murder sites is less than a quarter of an hour on foot, and the killings occurred within an hour of each other.

The first victim was discovered in a narrow passage off Burner Street, a thoroughfare connecting to Commercial Street. A carter, making his rounds in the early hours of the morning, stumbled upon the body around one o'clock. He found the woman lying lifeless, a deep gash across her throat, extending from ear to ear. Though deceased, her body, he reported, was still warm."

"Which suggests," I interjected, looking up from the paper, "that very little time had elapsed since the murder."

Holmes remained silent, his gaze fixed on some distant point, his face etched with a mixture of guilt and frustration. He was blaming himself, I knew, for not being there to prevent these latest tragedies.

I resumed reading, forcing my voice to remain steady, devoid of emotion.

34.

"Who is this mastermind, Holmes," I burst out, throwing the newspaper aside, unable to bear the oppressive silence any longer, "who has you so completely stymied, while he roams free, leaving a trail of carnage in his wake?" Holmes looked at me, startled by my outburst. It was clear, however, that the same question haunted him.

He gestured towards the bundle of clothing that lay discarded in the corner of the room, the one the constable had so carelessly tossed into our carriage. "Through this method, Watson, by immersing myself in the world of these unfortunate women, I gathered a wealth of information," he said, his voice low and intense.

"I believed," he continued, his gaze fixed on some distant point, "that I was close to unmasking this Ripper. Close to ending his reign of terror." He paused, his jaw clenching. I remained silent, the weight of his unspoken frustration pressing down on me. I poured myself a generous measure of brandy, the exhaustion of the day finally catching up with me.

"But my plans went awry," Holmes continued, his voice laced with bitterness. "Had I not been detained, those two women might still be alive. I might have caught the villain red-handed." He paced the room, his words tumbling out in a torrent of frustration.

"What now, Holmes?" I asked, my voice weary. "What do we do about these latest murders?"

"Lusk is seeking other counsel, Watson," he replied, his tone resigned. "And I can hardly blame him. He wants results, an end to this nightmare." He paused, a thoughtful frown creasing his brow.

"But what if there's more to it than that?" I ventured, voicing the suspicion that had been nagging at me. "There's something about Lusk, Holmes, something evasive. Do you not sense it as well?"

"There are forces at play here, Watson," Holmes murmured, his eyes narrowing, "forces we haven't yet grasped. Hidden agendas, secret alliances. I don't know who they are, but I intend to find out." His hand clenched into a fist, his knuckles white.

A chill ran down my spine. I drew closer to the warmth of the fireplace, seeking comfort in its flickering flames. Holmes joined me, not sitting, but leaning against the mantelpiece, his gaze lost in the dancing firelight.

After a long silence, he spoke, his voice low and thoughtful. "I spent many nights on those streets, Watson, shadowing suspects, observing the patterns of life in the shadows. The prostitutes, they move freely in that world, unseen, unheard by respectable society. It struck me as the perfect way to infiltrate that hidden realm." He paused, his eyes distant, as if reliving those nights. "I prepared myself in the carriage, with Lusk's trusted coachmen as my accomplices. It was Lusk who recommended them, vouched for their discretion. And so, the detective who boarded the carriage at Baker Street transformed into a woman of the night by the time we reached Leytonstone. From there, I walked to Whitechapel, alone, and immersed myself in the darkness."

He continued, his voice taking on a harder edge. "I encountered policemen, of course, and men with peculiar appetites. But for a time, I moved undetected. The true challenge, however, came from an unexpected quarter – the very women I sought to protect. It was unforeseen. Everything else was proceeding as planned. I'd identified several potential suspects, men who fit the profile, men I was watching closely. I even saw someone who matched the description of 'Leather Apron,' walking with a woman down a dimly lit street. He was a master of disguise, Watson, even more skilled than myself. It was only upon closer inspection that I realised it wasn't just a leather apron he wore..." He trailed off, his voice laced with a mixture of frustration and something akin to awe.

"What do you mean, Holmes?" I asked, my curiosity piqued.

Holmes sprang to his feet, a sudden energy animating his movements. He removed his coat, turning it inside out, and draped it over his chest, pulling the sleeves beneath his arms and tying them behind his back.

"Imagine, Watson," he began, "a coat made entirely of leather. Our man could transform it from a coat into an apron, and back again, in an instant. He commits the murder disguised as a man in a leather apron, then melts back into the crowd as a respectable gentleman, the blood-soaked lining concealed within. It allows him to reach a safe location, where he can dispose of the evidence and resume his normal guise."

"Not a leather apron, then," I mused, "but a leather coat. A reversible garment, easily concealed."

"Precisely!" Holmes exclaimed. "And that's exactly what I witnessed that night. I was tailing a man, about five foot three, with distinctly Jewish features, as he walked with a woman down a dimly lit street. I noticed the 'strings' tied behind his back weren't strings at all, but the sleeves of a coat. He seemed agitated, glancing over his shoulder repeatedly, as if he sensed he was being followed. I kept to the shadows, but just as I was closing in, I was interrupted." He sighed, the memory clearly still frustrating him.

"Those women, Watson, accosting me at such a crucial moment. The very people I was trying to protect became my undoing."

"It seems this 'Leather Apron' has little fear of the police," I observed.

"Indeed, Watson," Holmes replied, his eyes narrowing. "And isn't it curious that not a single individual matching that description has been apprehended yet?"

His arrest, coupled with this latest observation, reinforced the suspicion that someone, or something, was deliberately hindering the investigation.

"Still, Holmes," I offered, attempting to find a silver lining, "your arrest, unfortunate as it was, provides you with an alibi for these latest murders. It might have saved your reputation, perhaps even your life."

At the mention of his arrest, Holmes snatched up the bundle containing his discarded disguise and flung it into the fireplace.

"Two lives lost, Watson!" he cried, his voice thick with anguish. "Two women dead, while I sat in a cell!"

I knew better than to offer empty platitudes. Silently, I poked at the burning garments, the flames consuming the remnants of his ill-fated charade.

Holmes stood before the fireplace, his hands clasped behind his back, his gaze fixed on the dancing flames, as motionless as a marble statue. I saw the firelight reflected in his eyes, a burning intensity that made me look away. The physician in me recognized the signs of profound emotional exhaustion. I sighed, a quiet sound of shared weariness, and retreated to my chair, my own thoughts swirling in the smoke-filled air.

These murders defied easy explanation. Robbery was clearly not a motive, nor did it appear that the women themselves had played any part in their own demise. They were victims of circumstance, chance encounters in the dark streets of Whitechapel. There was no indication that the killer knew them beforehand.

Whether these were the acts of a madman, driven by an uncontrollable urge, or the calculated cruelty of a sane but depraved individual, one thing was certain: they were deliberate, intentional. But why? Was it a primal need to kill, a bloodlust that demanded satisfaction? What drew him to these women in particular? Was it their vulnerability, the ease with which they could be targeted? Or was it something more sinister, to satiate a cruel desire?

The escalating frequency of the murders, the chilling similarities between them, the audacity of the double killing on a Sunday morning – all pointed to a grim conclusion: this reign of terror was far from over.

35.

"Why Dorset Street, Holmes?" I asked, breaking the silence. "What drew you to that particular location?"

"Dorset Street, my dear Watson," Holmes replied, his voice regaining some of its usual crispness, "is the epicentre of iniquity in Spitalfields, arguably the most depraved slum in all of London. A festering sore on the face of this city." He paused, a flicker of disgust crossing his features. "It was once known as Datchet Street, named after William Wheeler, a landowner from Datchet who held the property a century ago. The name 'Dosset Street' evolved over time, perhaps corrupted by the presence of the numerous common lodging houses or 'doss houses', or simply mispronounced by the waves of immigrants who flocked to the area. One even hears it referred to as 'Dorsen Street' on occasion."

He continued, his voice taking on a more analytical tone. "A narrow thoroughfare, barely four hundred feet in length and a mere twenty-four feet wide runs north, parallel to Brushfield Street. To the south, it connects with White's Row. Crispin Street lies to the west, and Commercial Street to the east. A narrow passage, Paternoster Row, links Dorset Street with Brushfield Street, built, I believe, by one John Miller. It runs behind the houses of the more affluent residents. And at the far end, you'll find another alleyway, Miller's Court, which serves as a secondary entrance to Dorset Street."

"As I said, Dorset Street is riddled with lodging houses," Holmes continued, his voice taking on a harder edge. "Most operate under the control of Jack McCarthy and William Crossingham, the principal landowners. Both men are notorious for their involvement in a variety of illicit activities – smuggling, prostitution, gambling, and even human trafficking. It's a cesspool of vice, Watson, a breeding ground for every imaginable depravity." He paused, his lip curling in disgust.

"This is where one would find the lowest of the prostitutes in London. Most of the public houses are, in fact, brothels. From what I observed, there are only two legal establishments in that entire street; one is the shop owned by Mr. Barnet Price, the other, William Turner's Blue Coat Boy Club, which is actually a bar.

I found out that about one thousand and two hundred people take lodging for a night in these public houses on Dorset Street.

"My goodness!" I exclaimed, quite taken aback.

"Where Dorset Street intersects with Commercial Street," my companion continued, his voice crisp and analytical, "one finds The Britannia Club, formerly known as 'Ringers,' after its proprietor. It sits precisely opposite Millers' Court, with two of Crossingham's lodging houses a stone's throw away."

"Why are you burdening me with these details, Holmes?" I inquired, a touch of impatience creeping into my tone.

"Because, my dear Watson," he replied, a glint in his eye, "these seemingly disparate elements are, in fact, intricately interwoven."

"Annie Chapman," Holmes began, his voice low and thoughtful, "was last observed departing a public house, number 35, Dorset

Street. She then proceeded, if you'll recall, through Paternoster Row to Brushfield Street, and then towards Christchurch."

"A veritable rookery," I remarked, my lip curling in distaste. Holmes offered a curt nod of agreement.

"Indeed, Watson, a street full of whores." His choice of words, so blunt and uncharacteristic, startled me. It was clear that some simmering anger fueled his pronouncements, though its source remained a secret to me.

"There is a distinction to be made, I believe, Watson, between a prostitute and a whore, though you may disagree. The former retains a measure of youth and allure; the latter, ravaged by time and circumstance, possesses neither. They are, in the main, a wretched lot – helpless, impatient, cunning, their mouths drawn tight in a perpetual air of bashful defiance."

He paused, his gaze sweeping over the squalid scene. "The denizens of this street are well-matched to these women, Watson. One finds few Jews here, save perhaps the occasional Dutch Jew bold enough to venture into such a den of iniquity. No, it is our own countrymen who inhabit these shadows. Taverns abound, their doors swinging open to reveal scenes of drunken debauchery. Filthy shouts echo from every dwelling, the air thick with the stench of spirits and despair.

I observed Holmes closely, attempting to discern the wellspring of his words – was it profound understanding of these women, utter revulsion, or a potent blend of pity and disdain towards them?

"No God frequents these streets, Watson," he murmured, his voice tinged with a chilling solemnity. "This is the Devil's own domain."

Whatever tempest raged within him, it was clear that it exacted a heavy toll. In previous cases, the peril had been directed at a single individual. Here, however, a nebulous threat hung over an unidentified multitude, an uncertainty that chafed at Holmes's analytical mind.

I saw but one recourse. Though I abhorred his reliance upon the insidious drug, I knew that only cocaine could offer him the solace he so desperately craved. Retrieving his 7% solution and syringe from their hiding place, I placed them upon the teapoy, resolving to leave him to his own devices. I dared not broach the subject of the Whitechapel horrors again.

"I shall instruct Mrs. Hudson to have your dinner prepared for seven o'clock, Holmes," I said, moving towards the door. "And I shall inform her that you are not to be disturbed until then."

Ordinarily, he would have inquired as to my own intentions, but now he sat silent, his gaze fixed upon the flickering flames in the hearth. With a sigh, I closed the door behind me and descended the stairs, leaving him enveloped in the shadows of 221B. Stepping out onto Baker Street, I walked briskly away.

36.

The following morning, at Inspector Abberline's behest, we found ourselves at the Whitechapel police station, a scene of utter pandemonium. Though our arrival was noted, no one dared interrupt the inspector's furious dressing-down of the assembled constabulary. I occupied myself with a police gazette left upon a nearby table, quickly replacing it before Holmes could observe the lurid headlines detailing the double murder and the accompanying illustration of a man, dressed in female attire, being taken into custody.

"Murders committed within a stone's throw of each other," Abberline thundered, his voice echoing through the hall. "All victims of the unfortunate class. No witnesses, no sounds, no trace. Does this fiend simply vanish into thin air?"

"The people of this district, sir..." Officer Reid began, but Abberline cut him short, not letting his command over the station slip by.

"Silent they may be, but that does not render them normal. Deaf and blind, the lot of them!" The double murder, coupled with the indignity of Holmes's recent arrest, seemed to have galvanised the inspector. He was clearly determined to exert his authority, passing down the pressure from his superiors.

"These women, mutilated, should be lying in pools of their own blood! And the perpetrator, drenched in the blood of his victims! Where are the constables on their rounds? Are they bedding these women, while the killer makes his escape?" His roar hung in the air, met with a stony silence.

Indeed, the sheer impossibility of the villain's escapes lent credence to the whispers of supernatural agency. Was this the work of a phantom, or some bloodthirsty vampire, a human embodiment of pure evil?

"Why these women in particular?" I heard my companion's voice cut through the tension. "And why, with such horrors afoot, do they accompany their killer without protest?"

"A pertinent question," Abberline conceded. "It suggests familiarity, trust. Someone they would readily accompany." Holmes nodded in agreement, a silent exchange that did not go unnoticed by Officer Reid and his cohorts, their expressions darkening with resentment.

"A doctor, perhaps?" Reid ventured, his gaze shifting between myself and Lusk. "Or a priest?" He was well aware of my profession and Lusk's position within the church as a trustee.

"Precisely," Abberline replied, his eyes boring into Reid with the intensity of a hawk. "Someone wielding authority, someone respected within the community." Reid, sensing the danger, dropped his gaze. The implication hung heavy in the air, understood by all. Then, a young, naive officer, oblivious to the undercurrents, blurted out, "Perhaps it's one of us, then!"

Reid erupted. "This is no laughing matter! Who said that? Which imbecile?" He twisted in his seat, attempting to identify the speaker.

"This is precisely why we must question everyone in this district – man, woman, child, even the lunatic. Someone possesses knowledge they dare not divulge," Abberline declared, his voice ringing with authority. "Within three days, I expect each of you to have visited every dwelling, knocked on every door, taken detailed statements, and brought forth any individual warranting further scrutiny."

"Any questions?" He paused, met with silence. "Then get to it!" The constables dispersed, scurrying to obey his commands.

Once they had departed, Abberline approached us. "It's the only language they understand," he confided, a wry smile playing on his lips.

A map of Whitechapel adorned the far wall, dotted with red-headed pins marking the grim locations of the discovered bodies. As I studied the macabre cartography, Abberline drew Holmes aside, their conversation taking on a serious tone. Though loath to eavesdrop, I found myself drawn to their hushed exchange. They noticed my approach and shifted the subject, their practiced dissembling almost seamless.

"The Whitechapel Vigilance Committee hinders rather than helps our investigation," Abberline continued, his voice now pitched for my benefit. "How can we identify suspects when these amateur sleuths roam the streets? Were I the killer, I'd join their ranks, in the search of myself, the perfect disguise." He nodded a greeting in my direction.

Despite the absence of any constables, they persisted in their whispered discussion. I was thankful for Lusk's absence; Abberline's barely concealed antipathy towards the man was palpable. He clearly recognized the value of Holmes's involvement, ironically procured by Lusk, and was determined to offer his cooperation.

Holmes remained silent, his expression thoughtful, lost in contemplation.

As we departed the station, Abberline accompanied us, but Holmes offered no conversation, and I followed his lead. Just before we hailed a cab, however, Abberline placed a hand on Holmes's shoulder, leaning in conspiratorially.

"The Business Council's financial support stems not entirely from altruism," he murmured. "These crimes have crippled East London's economy. Any payment made to secure a resolution is not an expense, but an investment. This was discussed, I've learned, at a recent meeting at The Crown."

As the cab pulled away, Holmes, sensing my curiosity regarding their clandestine exchange, finally broke his silence.

"Abberline requires a list of the names comprising Lusk's Vigilance Committee," Holmes stated, his voice low and measured. "He intends to investigate each member."

"Indeed? And you acceded to this request?" I questioned, surprised.

"I did."

"But surely, Holmes, this constitutes a betrayal of Lusk's trust?"

"Not at all, Watson. Abberline's intentions are genuine. He seeks to uncover what we may have overlooked. He is, after all, the most capable mind at Scotland Yard."

"What leads you to such a conclusion?"

"During our private conversation, Abberline posited, 'Were I the perpetrator, I would infiltrate Lusk's committee, feigning assistance in my own apprehension.'"

I, too, recalled the inspector's words.

"Consider, Watson," Holmes continued, "the timing of these atrocities coincides precisely with the formation of the vigilance committee. Is it mere coincidence that the murders occur in such close proximity to their patrols? The second victim met her end directly in front of the Workers' meeting hall, while the committee was out on its rounds. Why, then, would Lusk, an intelligent man, not realise that the culprit might reside within his own ranks?"

His reasoning was compelling.

"Furthermore, Watson, you yourself observed the compromised nature of the evidence, deliberately obscured. I remarked upon this at the outset, noting the difficulty of drawing conclusions from evidence found in public spaces. Do you recollect my stating, on the very day Lusk sought our assistance, that were such a crime committed here on Baker Street, we would face similar challenges in gathering untainted evidence? With the vigilance committee patrolling the streets, how can we hope to isolate the true perpetrator? Abberline's concerns are well-founded."

"Do not ascribe every obstacle to Lusk, Holmes," I countered. "It was the police who apprehended you, not his committee. They were merely performing their duty." My words seemed to irritate him.

"It was the police who obliterated the evidence. They hindered your pursuit of the killer. It was the Police Commissioner himself who erased the murderer's message under cover of darkness."

Holmes's expression shifted, a flicker of recognition in his eyes. It was not a look of forgetfulness, but something else entirely, something I could not quite decipher. He seemed to be recalling something vital, something just beyond his grasp.

We paused in our conversation, casting a discreet glance towards our cab driver, ensuring our words remained private.

Lowering my voice to a whisper, mimicking the hushed tones of Holmes and Abberline at the station, I inquired, "Why would this individual incriminate himself with such a message? Why write anything at all, and not simply make good his escape?"

"Some, Watson, consider themselves above the law, convinced of their own invincibility. It is this ego that compels them to leave their mark," Holmes replied, his voice a low murmur.

"But what, Holmes, is the killer's objective? That remains a mystery."

"There is an objective, my dear fellow. No murder in the annals of crime has ever been without purpose." He paused, a thoughtful frown creasing his brow. Clearly, some thought preoccupied him, some deduction he was hesitant to share.

"These women were destitute," I pointed out, summarising the known facts. "Robbery cannot be the motive. Nor does revenge appear to be a factor. The medical reports rule out sexual assault. Why, then, the removal of organs?"

Holmes finally broke his silence, his voice tinged with a strange mixture of fascination and apprehension. "This case is different, Watson. Unique. There is a force at work here, something powerful."

"A secret society, perhaps?" I ventured.

Holmes merely smiled, a cryptic expression that offered no answers, only deepening the mystery.

37.

My notes on these grim affairs took on a decidedly scientific tone, a stark contrast to the romantic narratives Holmes had previously criticised. As I documented the events chronologically, it struck me that this objective style was best suited to chronicling such inexplicable occurrences. Though the narrative remained unfinished, I knew that to delay my record-keeping would be a disservice to the truth, and resolved to commit every detail to paper the very day it transpired.

"Isn't it a trifle premature to be chronicling the Whitechapel murders, Watson?" Holmes inquired from his accustomed place on the sofa, his pipe drawing contentedly.

Sensing an opportunity to glean further insights for my account, I replied, "I believe this case will be remembered as one of the most gruesome you have ever undertaken, Holmes. I can recall no other that comes close to matching its sheer horror."

A flicker of a satisfied smile crossed his lips before he quickly masked it.

"And yet, Watson, were I to request that you refrain from publishing this account, would you comply?" I rose from my chair, taken aback. Such a request was unprecedented. His expression brooked no argument. Could it be that he had already identified the culprit, and was withholding this knowledge from me?

"These are your adventures, Holmes," I conceded. "If you deem them unfit for publication, what right do I have to record them?"

He seemed to recognize the gravity of his request. Though a doctor by profession, my literary aspirations were inextricably linked to his exploits. I had once confessed that, thanks to him, writing might one day become my second calling. He surely remembered this.

"Very well," he sighed, a shadow passing over his features. "I shall divulge all that I know. Ask me anything you wish." He seemed determined to dispel the gloom that had settled upon us.

"Why Whitechapel, Holmes?" I inquired. "London is a vast metropolis, Britain a sprawling empire. Why this particular district?"

He paced before the sofa, gathering his thoughts. "Whitechapel is notorious throughout London for its illicit activities. Dean Street and Flower Street are considered amongst the most dangerous thoroughfares in the city. Dorset Street, in fact, bears the unenviable title of 'the worst street in London.' It is a breeding ground for robbery, debauchery, and violence."

"Furthermore," he continued, "the district is mired in poverty. The housing is substandard, sanitation is practically non-existent. Homelessness, drunkenness, and prostitution are rampant. Consider this, Watson: in the capital city of an empire upon which the sun never sets, in this eastern corner of London, Whitechapel alone boasts two hundred and thirty-three public houses. Eight thousand five hundred souls seek nightly lodging within their walls."

"Those who inhabit these establishments are the lost and the forgotten, the aimless and the desperate. A bed can be had for four pence a night. For a mere two pence, an adult or child can find a space to lie down, but not to sleep."

"The victims of these atrocities are drawn from this very community, Watson. Specifically, the identified victims hail from the heart of this darkness – Spitalfields. While the press, no doubt, sensationalised the initial killings to boost their circulation, I do not believe all can be attributed to the single Whitechapel murderer we seek. However, the last four bear distinct similarities, the unmistakable hallmarks of the same hand. The notoriety of the earlier murders undoubtedly emboldened this fiend."

"The police," I remarked, my voice laced with frustration, "have utterly failed in their duty to protect the citizenry. Their hasty obliteration of evidence, the cleansing of the crime scenes, and the indignity they subjected you to, beggars belief. Whatever respect I once held for the constabulary has vanished entirely. Furthermore, I sense that Inspector Abberline lacks the support of his own force. It seems that only you and Lusk's Vigilance Committee offer him any true assistance."

Holmes nodded gravely, confirming my assessment.

38.

Lusk had initially sought Holmes's aid due to the constabulary's utter failure to uncover any meaningful evidence. Yet, we were aware that he and his Vigilance Committee had also engaged the services of another detective, a certain Le Grand. Lusk had been curiously reticent about this individual, offering neither introduction nor details of his involvement. Holmes, for his part, made no inquiries on the matter.

Holmes, however, had now firmly established his deductive prowess, silencing both Lusk and the previously dismissive police. Even Abberline, initially resistant to collaborating with a private detective, now deferred to Holmes's judgement, acknowledging his superior skills.

Meanwhile, Le Grand had proposed a novel approach to reviving Abberline's earlier, unsuccessful attempt to utilise bloodhounds. He had identified the flaws in the previous operation, and the police, eager for any promising lead, were prepared to implement his revised strategy.

Following Le Grand's instructions, a fabricated narrative, a veritable fairytale, was disseminated amongst the populace on the eve of the operation. This carefully crafted deception served to mask the true nature of the police undertaking.

Deploying bloodhounds to track an unknown killer in Whitechapel was akin to playing with fire. History offered ample warning of the potential consequences.

This time, however, Le Grand's concocted tale preceded the operation. Abberline, shrewdly following Le Grand's counsel, dispatched plainclothes officers, strategically placed within various social strata, to subtly propagate the story.

I confess, a pang of professional jealousy struck me. Le Grand, it seemed, possessed a narrative flair that surpassed my own. Yet, his story, proving instrumental to the operation and yielding valuable intelligence, demanded inclusion in this chronicle. Therefore, I shall dutifully record it here.

The fabricated narrative painted a picture of George Dodge, a sailor with an alleged talent for Malay cookery. He was portrayed as a naive young man, deeply smitten with a woman of ill repute who had exploited his affections and, ultimately, robbed him of his fortune during his sojourn in London. Driven to despair by her betrayal, Dodge vowed revenge upon all women of her profession.

This carefully constructed tale, now disseminated amongst the public, positioned Dodge as the prime suspect in the Whitechapel atrocities. His shipmates, it was claimed, had recently returned from sea and revealed that Dodge, in a drunken fit of rage, had sworn to avenge himself upon such women, vowing to kill and mutilate them until he found the one who had wronged him. This information, it was explained, had only just come to light upon the sailors' return. Dodge, upon reaching port, had abandoned his comrades, leaving them horrified by his apparent commitment to his drunken oath.

The public, now primed with this compelling narrative, readily accepted the explanation that the bloodhounds were being employed to track down the vengeful George Dodge.

"A most ingenious fabrication," Holmes remarked to Abberline, admiring the cleverness of the narrative. "It allows the operation to proceed without inciting undue alarm amongst the populace. This Le Grand appears to possess a remarkable talent for storytelling. Perhaps, Lusk," he turned to the committee chairman, "you might introduce him to my friend, Watson?" Lusk, accepting the compliment with a thin smile, offered no reply.

The following day, a large-scale operation commenced. Bloodhounds, their noses to the ground, sniffed at the murder sites and the victims' belongings, their paths crisscrossing the streets of Whitechapel. Police officers and constables conducted house-to-house inquiries, diligently recording statements.

Despite the extensive effort, Inspector Abberline appeared dejected upon his subsequent visit to Baker Street.

"The dogs have covered every street in Whitechapel," he reported, his voice heavy with disappointment.

He produced a sheaf of notes, detailing the routes taken by each hound and its handler, precisely as Holmes had requested. At my companion's signal, I unfurled the map of Whitechapel upon my writing desk.

For over an hour and a half, we pored over the map, tracing the routes of the bloodhounds with our fingers, our voices a low murmur of speculation and deduction as we cross-referenced Abberline's notes. At last, a pattern emerged, clear and undeniable.

"Mr. Abberline, observe," Holmes said, his voice sharp with excitement. "The hounds have repeatedly converged upon these three streets." He pointed to a specific section of the map.

"Fieldgate Street, Middlesex Street, and Whitechapel Street," Abberline confirmed, his voice hushed.

Holmes drew a circle, encompassing the three streets and the surrounding area most frequented by the hounds. "Our quarry resides within this perimeter," he declared, tapping the circle emphatically.

Abberline's jaw slackened in astonishment, but his eyes gleamed with a newfound sense of purpose.

"Deploy your officers to search this area," Holmes instructed. "Seek out an individual matching the description I have provided."

Chief Inspector Abberline, charged with the daunting task of apprehending the Whitechapel murderer, nodded resolutely.

We watched from the window as Abberline strode confidently towards his waiting carriage on Baker Street. Watching him, Holmes perched himself upon the window sill, and reached for his violin.

39.

The investigation, reinvigorated by Holmes's deduction, took on a renewed urgency. The pressure upon the police, intensified by the four brutal murders, remained palpable.

At Abberline's invitation, Holmes and I attended a review meeting the following day at the Whitechapel police station.

"We have compiled dossiers on every surgeon, butcher, cook, and barber residing within a ten-mile radius of the designated area,"

Abberline announced, his voice strained with the weight of the unsolved crimes. "Every man in Whitechapel has been questioned – Jew, German, and Frenchman. Our officers have searched high and low, yet the fiend remains at large. Someone, somewhere, possesses knowledge vital to this case. We must uncover it!" His voice rose to a roar of frustration.

The assembled constables sat in stony silence, their faces grim. Even Officer Reid had taken his place amongst the ranks, a clear indication that Abberline had reasserted his authority.

"We must distribute these pamphlets," Abberline declared, gesturing towards a stack of printed warnings. "The public must be made aware of the danger before this predator strikes again."

"But sir," a constable ventured, his voice hesitant, "what if the villain has already fled to the countryside?"

"My concern," Abberline stated coldly, fixing the constable with a steely gaze before letting his eyes sweep over the assembled men, "is limited to this district. However," he continued, his voice taking on a sharper edge, "you gentlemen should be aware that half of Europe, not to mention our American cousins across the Atlantic, are watching this drama unfold with bated breath. Everything we say and do here becomes fodder for their newspapers. Each of you has been assigned a section. You will be held accountable for what transpires within it. Now go!"

Once the constables had dispersed, Abberline approached us. We had taken our customary positions at the rear of the hall. He drew a chair up before us, his earlier fury seemingly dissipated.

Looking around to ensure our privacy, he leaned towards Holmes, his voice low and confidential.

"Holmes," he murmured, "something about this case doesn't ring true."

"And what, pray tell, is that?" Holmes inquired, his eyes narrowing.

At that very moment, Lusk's carriage drew up outside the station, but Abberline, eager to share his thoughts before Lusk's arrival, pressed on.

"I believe," he confided, glancing pointedly at me, "that we are dealing with more than one individual." I understood that his words were not directed at myself.

"If that is indeed the case," I ventured, "what, then, is the connection between them?" Abberline, however, kept his gaze fixed upon Holmes.

"That, my dear Watson," he replied, "is a puzzle best left to Holmes's superior intellect."

It was clear that Abberline, like myself, awaited Holmes's deductions with a mixture of anticipation and apprehension. My companion, however, remained lost in thought, his brow furrowed in concentration.

Meanwhile, Lusk approached, accompanied by two other gentlemen. As they drew nearer, I recognized the familiar figure of Dr. Llewellyn. The other, I surmised, was Joseph Aaron, the treasurer of the Vigilance Committee.

Lusk carried a package and a letter, but it was Aaron's expression, a mixture of anxiety and grim determination, that suggested these were no ordinary correspondence.

Lusk placed the package upon Abberline's desk and stepped back.

"This arrived at my residence yesterday by post," he explained, his voice trembling slightly. "I took it for a morbid jest and placed it in my desk drawer. I informed the committee of its existence at our meeting this morning." He gestured towards the package, but no one moved to touch it.

Mr. Joseph Aaron then spoke, his tone grave. "I, along with Harry, Reeves, and Lorton, went to Lusk's home immediately upon hearing this news to examine the package. He was reluctant to trouble us, but we are deeply concerned for his safety. The leadership he has shown in protecting our community has placed him in considerable danger. This is a most serious matter. We urged him to consult a physician, and suggested Dr. Frederick Willis."

"Dr. Willis's surgery being in Mile End Road," Lusk continued, "I followed their advice. However, the doctor was absent. His assistant examined the package and recommended we consult Dr. Thomas Horrocks Openshaw at the London Hospital. But we decided to present it to the committee first. Dr. Llewellyn kindly agreed to join us and offer his expertise. We have come here directly from that meeting."

"For heaven's sake," Abberline exclaimed, his patience clearly wearing thin, "will someone tell me what this blasted package contains?!"

Dr. Llewellyn stepped forward, his face grim, and carefully untied the string securing the package. He lifted the lid, revealing the gruesome contents within.

"A human kidney," he announced, his voice hushed.

Though Llewellyn identified the organ, preserved in a jar of alcohol, as a kidney, it was, in fact, only a portion of one.

"The letter was positioned so as to be immediately visible upon opening the box," Lusk explained, handing a folded piece of paper to Holmes with a trembling hand. "It was addressed to me personally. The package was delivered to my residence at Number 1, Alderney Road, Mile End. I discovered both the letter and…this, upon opening it."

I took the letter from Holmes and read its contents aloud.

From hell

Mr Lusk

Sor
I send you half the
Kidne I took from one women
prasarved it for you tother piece I
fried and ate it was very nise I
may send you the bloody knif that
took it out if you only wate a whil
longer

Signed   Catch me when
you can
Mishter Lusk

"From hell

Mr Lusk

Sor

I send you half the Kidne I took from one women prasarved it for you tother pirce I fried and ate it was very nise I may send you the bloody knif that took it out if you only wate a whil longer.

signed Catch me when

you Can

Mishter Lusk."

All eyes were fixed upon the grisly exhibit before us.

"Why was this letter addressed to Lusk?" Abberline questioned, his brow furrowed. "All previous correspondence has been directed to the newspapers."

"I've noticed a rather sinister-looking fellow with a beard loitering near my residence since late August," Lusk replied, his voice tinged with anxiety. "I even requested police protection from Officer Reid, but he dismissed my concerns."

Holmes turned to Dr. Llewellyn. "Tell me, Doctor, does such precise dissection require surgical skill?"

"Must you persist in implicating the medical profession, Mr. Holmes?" Llewellyn retorted, his voice rising slightly. "A butcher performs similar dissections daily." His tone betrayed a wounded professional pride.

"Very well, gentlemen," Abberline interjected, sensing the rising tension. "I shall look into this matter." He dismissed Lusk and his companions, then turned back to us.

"This preserved kidney fragment, along with this 'letter from hell'," Abberline began, his voice low and thoughtful, "was sent directly to Lusk on the sixteenth of October. The postmark indicates it was sent the day prior. Yet, he chose to present it to us only today." His suspicion of Lusk was visible.

Holmes, roused from his contemplation, addressed Abberline. "You'll note, Inspector that unlike the letters sent to the newspapers, this one bears the unmistakable hallmarks of the murderer himself." He paused, as if searching for a specific detail.

"Indeed," Abberline agreed. "It lacks the signature, 'Jack the Ripper,' so prevalent in the newspaper correspondence."

Holmes's voice took on a sharper edge, indicating that Abberline had missed the salient point. "What murderer in his right mind would sign a confession with his own name? This letter cannot be the fabrication of a journalist, precisely because it omits the moniker 'Jack the Ripper,' so readily employed by the press to sensationalise these crimes."

"People do write such preposterous letters to the newspapers," Abberline conceded. "They imagine themselves witty, though I fail to see the humour."

"Lusk, as you know, chairs the Vigilance Committee tasked with apprehending this Ripper," Holmes mused, pacing the room. "He, along with the other members of the committee, composed of local businessmen, was appointed on the tenth of September. From that point forward, Lusk's name was plastered all over Whitechapel as the point of contact for anyone possessing information regarding the murderer. It strikes me as odd that, given the speed with which the previous letters were dispatched to the press, it took so long for this one to reach Lusk directly."

He paused, his brow furrowed in thought. "And yet," he continued, turning to us, "upon examining this letter, a singular detail struck me. I believe you, too, will have observed it." He looked at us expectantly, but I could recall nothing remarkable about the missive.

Abberline, equally perplexed, frowned in concentration.

Suddenly, Holmes's eyes lit up with a flash of inspiration. He waved the red-inked "letter from hell" triumphantly before us.

"Gentlemen, don't you see?" he exclaimed, his voice ringing with excitement. "The handwriting is identical to that found upon the wall! Furthermore, the grammatical and spelling errors precisely mirror those we observed in the graffiti. I am convinced that both were penned by the same hand. This, gentlemen, is the work of the Whitechapel murderer!"

40.

The streets of London, like the veins and arteries of some vast, slumbering beast, conceal a multitude of secrets.

From the quiet country lanes that snake their way into the city's heart, to the grim, shadowed alleys that crisscross its underbelly, every thoroughfare has borne witness to humanity's darker impulses – cruelty, violence, jealousy, and the bitter ashes of extinguished hope. Crimes of passion and cold-blooded murder have stained their cobblestones. They have watched as villains slipped the grasp of justice, while others, innocent or guilty, and were ensnared in its unforgiving web.

But the continued freedom of the Whitechapel fiend cast a pall over London, a chill that pierced deeper than the encroaching winter's bite. No other season had held the city in such thrall as the Autumn of Terror, 1888. A creeping dread, heavier than the fog that clung to the gas lit streets, settled upon the hearts of its inhabitants. Then, after a six-week respite since the double murder – a horror we had, until then, considered unsurpassed – an even more gruesome atrocity unfolded.

It was apparent that the reign of terror was far from over.

In November, another telegram arrived from Lusk, bearing news of yet another murder. Holmes, having read the message first, observed my crestfallen expression in sympathy.

He approached my desk and waited patiently for me to cease my writing and acknowledge his presence. I laid down my pen and looked up.

"Watson," he began, his voice low and serious, "you once inquired as to my reasons for focusing our attention upon Dorset Street. Your question has now been answered. My supposition was correct. Jack the Ripper resides in that very vicinity. See for yourself." He handed me the telegram.

"Another terrible murder on Dorset Street – Lusk," I read aloud, my voice barely a whisper. I snatched the telegram from Holmes's hand, rereading the stark message, scarcely able to comprehend its dreadful import.

"Yesterday, the ninth of November," I stammered, "a woman was brutally murdered at Miller's Court, Dorset Street, Spitalfields."

"Dorset Street!" I exclaimed, turning to Holmes, my mind reeling. "You were right, Holmes! I now understand the significance of your observations that day. You pinpointed the location with uncanny accuracy."

Holmes, however, did not share my excitement. He sank into the chair beside my desk, a heavy sigh escaping his lips. He sat hunched over, his fingers laced together between his knees, his gaze fixed upon the floor.

As I reread the telegram, Holmes's vivid description of Dorset Street resurfaced in my memory, now imbued with a chilling prescience.

Unfortunately, a prior commitment to a gravely ill patient prevented me from accompanying Holmes to the scene. My duties as a physician, always paramount, took precedence over even the most compelling of investigations. Having attended to my patient, I returned to Baker Street, my mind heavy with the news of the latest atrocity.

Holmes returned late that night, his face drawn and pale.

"The victim at Miller's Court, Watson," he began, his voice weary, "a Mary Jane Kelly, was, as I suspected, a frequenter of the Britannia Club – the establishment formerly known as 'Ringers,' if you recall. She was a familiar face there, and it is highly probable that Jack the Ripper encountered her at that very location. She was, after all, murdered at Miller's Court, situated directly opposite."

Holmes's uncharacteristic loquaciousness, in contrast to his haggard appearance, suggested the influence of some stimulant. However, I refrained from commenting. The pallor of his face and the haunted look in his eyes spoke of a deeper distress that transcended mere chemical stimulation. I saw a genuine anguish in his gaze.

"I had believed, Watson," he began, his voice tinged with a wistful sadness, "that Jack the Ripper's bloodlust had been sated with the deaths of Elizabeth Stride and Catherine Eddowes. Despite our failure to apprehend him, I was relieved that the murders had ceased." He turned towards me, his eyes glistening with unshed tears. I feared that the prolonged strain of the case was pushing him towards the brink of a nervous breakdown.

Even the cheerful blaze in the hearth could not dispel the chill that had settled upon us. We sat in silence, enveloped by the growing cold of the Baker Street sitting room.

"But yesterday," Holmes continued, his voice barely above a whisper, "six weeks after the double murder, a twenty-five-year-old prostitute, Mary Jane Kelly, was found mutilated upon her own bed."

The expression on Holmes's face told me that I had been spared a truly horrific sight.

"I have witnessed nothing so gruesome in all my days, Watson," he confessed, his voice thick with revulsion, fighting back a wave of nausea. "Her entrails…they were upon the ceiling."

My legs gave way, and I collapsed onto the nearest chair. I braced myself for what I knew would be a description of unimaginable depravity.

"Such savagery…it defies human comprehension. Such an act cannot be committed by one who calls himself human," Holmes murmured, his voice choked with emotion. "My God, Watson, Mary Kelly…she was so young, so full of life…" His voice cracked, and a sob escaped his lips, quickly stifled by a sharp intake of breath. He brushed away the tears with the back of his hand.

His composure, so meticulously maintained, seemed to crumble before my eyes. His mind, I knew, would be reprimanding him for such an uncharacteristic display of emotion. Yet, in that moment of vulnerability, his essential humanity shone through.

I silently proffered the brandy decanter and a glass.

He offered a fleeting look of gratitude, but his eyes remained clouded with a despair I had never witnessed before.

Ignoring the glass, he lifted the decanter to his lips and took two long draughts of the fiery liquid, as if seeking to extinguish some inner inferno.

I waited patiently, allowing him the time he needed to compose himself. His anguish was contagious, a palpable presence in the room. I had never known Holmes to express such profound empathy, such visceral distress for another human being.

Finally, after several minutes of heavy silence, he spoke, his voice halting and strained.

"Kelly was last seen alive around two o'clock in the morning," Holmes recounted, his voice flat and devoid of inflection.

"Witnesses report that she had entertained two clients earlier in the evening. I examined her room. Her clothes and boots were neatly arranged, suggesting she had been preparing for sleep. But sleep never came."

He paused, his breath catching in his throat. "When we arrived, her entrails, they were arranged around her body, like some grotesque banquet. Her face was so savagely mutilated as to be unrecognisable. One breast, a kidney, and her lungs were placed beneath her head. The other kidney lay to her left. Upon a nearby table, her thigh and other viscera. Her ribcage was empty. Her heart was missing. And, as in previous cases, her womb had been removed."

He shuddered, the memory clearly vivid and abhorrent. "I fled the room, gasping for air. Lusk, Abberline, and I, we had nothing to say. They had no questions, and I...I had no answers. I went directly to indulge in my habit."

His words painted a picture of such unmitigated horror that I could scarcely bear to listen. To have witnessed such a scene firsthand...I shuddered to think of the toll it must have taken on Holmes's psyche.

"Catherine Eddowes's face was similarly mutilated, if you recall," I remarked, my voice barely above a whisper. "It would seem that Jack has returned."

Holmes looked at me, a strange expression on his face, as if he disagreed with my assessment.

"A casual observer," Holmes stated, his voice low and intense, "would undoubtedly conclude that this latest atrocity bears the hallmarks of the previous four, and proclaim the return of Jack the Ripper. But that, my dear Watson, is not the case."

I stared at him, bewildered. Could his recent indulgence have clouded his judgement?

"This murder," he continued, "exhibits significant deviations from the established pattern. The previous four were committed in public spaces, this one within the confines of a private residence. The others were executed with swift, brutal efficiency, while this…this act of barbarism suggests a lingering, a savouring of the process."

"And yet," I countered, "the killer has once again claimed his gruesome trophy – the womb."

"True," Holmes conceded, "but the womb is not the only organ missing, Watson. The heart, too, is absent. This is significant!" His eyes gleamed with a sudden intensity, as if the missing organ had unlocked some vital piece of the puzzle. He seemed to be visualising the killer, the image coalescing before his very eyes.

"This detail alone," he emphasised, "sets this murder apart. The sheer extent of the mutilation surpasses anything we have seen before. This is not simply another murder, Watson. This is something else entirely." He repeated the words, "Different. Special."

"A cursory examination of the crime scene suggests that the victim was acquainted with her murderer," Holmes continued, his voice regaining some of its customary analytical detachment. "The mutilation of her face was not a haphazard act, as in the case of Eddowes. It was a deliberate attempt to prevent identification. This, coupled with the fact that a cloth had been placed over her face before the attack, strongly suggests a prior relationship. He covered her face because he could not bear to look upon her as he committed this unspeakable act. He must have acted in a frenzy, oblivious to the extent of the damage he was inflicting."

"Moreover, Watson, her clothes were neatly folded upon a chair in the corner of the room. Why this meticulous tidiness? It suggests that she was expecting a visitor, someone she considered respectable. A prostitute would hardly bother with such domestic niceties when receiving a regular client."

"Even if we entertain the notion that Mary Kelly lured Jack the Ripper to her room," Holmes reasoned, "this detail remains incongruous. Jack is a creature of impulse, driven by a primal fury. He kills with a swift, brutal passion, taking his victims by surprise. The fact that her clothes were so carefully arranged suggests that this was not his handiwork."

"Perhaps she disrobed completely," I suggested, pondering the implications. "Or worse…perhaps the man observed her as she undressed, waited for her to retire to bed, and then struck." Holmes nodded slowly, acknowledging the plausibility of my theory.

"If she was clad only in her nightgown," he mused, "it implies that she willingly admitted someone into her room. A woman would only do so for someone she knew and trusted. Something must have gone terribly wrong after that, leading to this."

41.

The entirety of Scotland Yard, under the watchful eye of Chief Inspector Robert Anderson, convened to deliberate their next course of action. A palpable sense of determination hung in the air; these brutal killings must be brought to an end.

Scotland Yard, as the nerve centre of London's constabulary, had amassed a considerable body of evidence. Frederick Abberline, heading the Ripper investigation, presented Holmes with a comprehensive file detailing their findings.

Within its pages, a list of suspects had been compiled, each individual deemed a potential candidate for the mantle of "Jack the Ripper." All, I noted, aligned with Holmes's earlier pronouncements.

Abberline meticulously outlined each suspect's name and description, while Holmes listened with rapt attention, his keen mind dissecting every detail.

He spent a considerable time poring over the file, separating certain documents from the rest, returning some to Abberline while retaining others. Suddenly, as he perused a particular document, he froze, his body stiffening as if struck by a bolt of lightning.

He looked up, his gaze sweeping over the assembled faces, a triumphant smile playing at the corners of his lips. A shiver ran down my spine.

"I have maintained from the outset," he announced, his voice ringing with conviction, "that only a butcher could have committed the initial murders." He held aloft the document in his hand. "Who else could move freely amongst the public, unperturbed, with bloodstains upon their attire? Upon my suggesting this to Abberline, he instructed his men to pursue this line of inquiry."

Abberline nodded in confirmation.

"This particular suspect," Holmes continued, his voice laced with a hint of recrimination, "appears to have been overlooked by the police. I find this surprising, given your familiarity with the individual. Of all the names on your list, he is the one upon whom I placed the greatest suspicion."

He presented the document to Chief Inspector Anderson.

"His name, gentlemen," Holmes declared, his voice resonating with authority, "is Jacob Levy!"

42.

It was not Holmes's custom to reveal his methods prematurely. He relished the astonishment of his audience when, at the culmination of a case, he unveiled the solution to the mystery. However, in this instance, he seemed eager to expound upon his reasoning.

"Jacob Levy is a butcher," he explained, "and also a Jew. He aligns perfectly with the profile I have constructed of our killer," Holmes declared, a touch of self-satisfaction in his tone.

"You may now appreciate, gentlemen," Holmes continued, addressing the assembled officers, "that my method of deducing the criminal based on the established pattern of the crimes is a most effective, and indeed, intelligent course of action."

He then retrieved the annotated map of Whitechapel from the dossier, the one Abberline and I had helped him to mark. The circle Holmes had drawn, encompassing the murder sites and the routes most frequented by the bloodhounds, stood out starkly. He spread the map upon the table for all to see.

"This individual," Holmes declared, his voice ringing with authority, "not only conforms to my profile in terms of ethnicity and profession, but also satisfies another crucial criterion – proximity. I have become increasingly convinced over the past months that the killer must operate within this specific area, close to the locations of the murders. He is either a resident, or a frequent visitor."

"Observe, gentlemen that Jacob Levy resides on Fieldgate Street, and his butcher shop is located on Middlesex Street. Both fall squarely within the demarcated area – the hunting ground, if you will, of Jack the Ripper."

He paused for effect, allowing his words to sink in. "Consider the advantages afforded by a lockable meat stall. Such a location would provide an ideal repository for his 'trophies'. Imagine the convenience, gentlemen, for Jacob Levy to have a butcher shop on Middlesex Street, at the very heart of his operations. He could cleanse himself at his leisure before returning home. I could have kicked myself, gentlemen, when I realised I held in my possession a statement from Levy's wife!" He snatched up another document from the table, his eyes gleaming with triumph.

"I find it astonishing," Holmes continued, his voice laced with incredulity, "that the police overlooked this crucial piece of evidence while we were tirelessly searching for clues."

He referred to the document in hand. "In her statement, Mrs. Levy describes her husband as mentally unstable, and confesses to difficulties in their marriage. She attributes the failing state of his business to his negligence, and states quite plainly that he neglects his butcher shop, preferring to roam the streets at night for reasons unknown to her."

He paused, his expression thoughtful. "While this statement alone does not constitute sufficient grounds for an arrest, it certainly warrants further investigation. I therefore made inquiries into Mr. Levy's past. Prior to these murders, he was accused of stealing meat from his clients. While this may appear to be a petty crime, the act of stealing meat aligns with the profile of a killer who mutilates his victims and removes their organs. Such individuals often exhibit a pattern of dishonesty, even in seemingly insignificant matters. Lying without cause, cheating for minimal gain, even petty theft - these are all indicative of a deeper moral depravity."

"You may recall, gentlemen," Holmes continued, "the murder committed in Hanbury Street, in the garden belonging to Mrs. Richardson. She employed several men at her pet food shop. Upon further investigation, I discovered that approximately one month prior to the murder, Mrs. Thompson, the wife of one of Mrs. Richardson's employees, observed a man sleeping upon the stairs in that very garden. It was around four o'clock in the morning. She described him as Jewish, with a distinctly foreign accent.

"When questioned as to his purpose there, he claimed to be merely resting until the market opened. He had apparently spent the night upon the stairs. I believe, in fact, that he had made a habit of sleeping there. Mrs. Thompson expressed confidence in her ability to identify the man, based on both his appearance and his distinctive manner of speech."

"We then enlisted the assistance of the renowned artist, Walter Sickert," Holmes continued, his voice tinged with a hint of pride. "Mr. Sickert, as you know, has taken a keen interest in these murders, and his artistic skill is unsurpassed. We therefore put his talents to good use in our investigation."

"I discreetly escorted Mrs. Thompson to Mr. Sickert's studio, where she provided a detailed description of the suspect. Mr. Sickert, with his remarkable ability to capture a likeness, produced a portrait of the individual we believe to be Jack the Ripper. I then circulated this portrait amongst those who claimed to have seen the killer, or who were likely to have encountered him. This was done with the utmost secrecy, of course."

"Amongst the statements gathered, one in particular caught my attention. The proprietor of the public house at Number 30, Dorset Street, in his account following the murder of Annie Chapman, mentioned that Chapman had been a regular patron some two years prior. She frequently arrived in the company of a man named 'Jack Sivvy,' so called because of his profession as a sieve-maker. He further stated that Chapman, being Sivvy's lover, was sometimes known as 'Annie Sivvy.'" Holmes retrieved the portrait from the file and presented it to the assembled officers.

"And this, my dear Chief Inspector Anderson," he declared, his voice ringing with triumph, "is none other than Jacob Levy!"

Inspector Anderson, having listened intently to Holmes's meticulous explanation, nodded slowly.

"It is evident, then," Holmes concluded, "that 'Jack Sivvy' is, in fact, Jacob Levy. The diminutive 'Jack' is a common variant of 'Jacob,' and the surname 'Sivvy' could easily be misheard as 'Levy,' particularly given the fluid nature of nomenclature in a district like Whitechapel. We are all familiar with the various appellations Dorset Street has acquired over the years."

Only then did the full scope of Holmes's investigation become apparent, even to me. The assembled detectives and the Commissioner himself were visibly astonished. Only Abberline, perhaps due to his closer involvement with the case, maintained a semblance of composure.

Holmes, however, had not yet finished. "With the assistance of a physician attached to the syphilis clinic at the London Hospital," he continued, "I examined their patient registry to further corroborate my findings. I was not surprised, gentlemen, to discover Jacob Levy's name amongst those receiving treatment for this social disease. He had contracted the illness, despite being a married man with children, presumably through his association with the prostitutes of Whitechapel."

"Furthermore," he added, his voice dropping to a conspiratorial whisper, "his medical records indicate auditory hallucinations – voices, he claims, that compel him to commit certain acts. Such hallucinations, coupled with irrational impulses, are a hallmark of advanced syphilis."

43.

"I recently paid a visit to Butcher's Row, seeking Jacob Levy," Holmes continued, his voice taking on a thoughtful tone. "There, gentlemen, I encountered a certain Joseph Hyam Levy, a Jewish businessman, and, significantly, one of the three witnesses who observed Eddowes in the company of her killer. His initial statement proved unremarkable; he claimed to be unable to identify the man. However, upon further conversation, his demeanour suggested otherwise. His expressions betrayed a familiarity with the killer, a knowledge he was clearly withholding. It struck me, gentlemen, that any attempt to describe Jacob Levy to this young man would be superfluous; he was almost certainly a relative. It also became apparent that Jacob Levy was deliberately avoiding me, as he was conspicuously absent from his butcher shop whenever I subsequently called."

He paused, his eyes narrowing. "Joseph Levy's marked disinterest in providing a description of the potential killer further aroused my suspicions. This reluctance, I surmised, stemmed from the fact that he had recognized the man. And that man, gentlemen, is none other than Jacob Levy."

"Both men are butchers, their stalls situated side-by-side in Butcher's Row," Holmes explained. "Joseph Levy's stall is less than fifty yards from Jacob's. This proximity, I believe, accounts for Joseph's reticence. He possessed information that incriminated his colleague, yet chose to remain silent. However, unwittingly, he did offer a crucial piece of information to the police. Though they dismissed it as insignificant, it pointed directly, in my view, to Jacob Levy."

Holmes, with the flourish of a barrister presenting his case, produced another document from the file.

"Joseph Levy stated that Jack the Ripper was three inches taller than Catherine Eddowes. Jacob Levy stands at five feet three inches. The deceased, Catherine Eddowes, was five feet tall. A perfect match!"

"The police, however, disregarded this vital clue, deeming it contradictory to the statements of the other two witnesses. Those witnesses, gentlemen, offered only estimations of the killer's height, whereas Joseph Levy provided a precise difference in height relative to the victim. Surely, a comparative measurement is inherently more reliable than a mere guess? I find it baffling that this point needs clarification for the esteemed officers of Scotland Yard." A hint of sarcasm crept into Holmes's voice.

"With such compelling evidence pointing towards Jacob Levy's guilt," he concluded, turning to Chief Inspector Anderson, "I am astonished that the police have failed to act. While I know that nothing can restore these unfortunate women to life, this monster must be stopped before he claims another victim." His voice rang with urgency.

44.

The weight of evidence presented by Holmes, so meticulously gathered and so logically presented, was undeniable. Chief Inspector Anderson, along with the other assembled officers, recognised the compelling nature of the case against Jacob Levy. With more evidence pointing towards his guilt than any other suspect, Commissioner Anderson, with the authorisation of Magistrate Saunders of the Thames Police Court, issued a warrant for Levy's arrest.

The operation was shrouded in secrecy, entrusted solely to Scotland Yard under Abberline's command. At Abberline's specific request, Holmes was to accompany the arresting officers, his keen eye essential for positive identification of the suspect. And I, as always, accompanied my friend, my trusty revolver at my side.

The operation to apprehend Jacob Levy that very night was planned with utmost discretion, orchestrated by Holmes and Abberline.

We assembled at the Lyceum Theatre, at Holmes's suggestion, to while away the hours before the planned arrest. While intended as a diversion, the performance, for me, only served to amplify my anxieties.

I have never fully grasped the art of theatrical impersonation, the ability of an actor to inhabit a character so completely. As I watched Richard Mansfield's masterful portrayal of the dual personalities of Dr. Jekyll and Mr. Hyde, I found myself pondering whether our Whitechapel fiend might possess similar transformative powers. The ease with which Mansfield shifted from gentleman to monster, before our very eyes, was both mesmerising and unsettling.

What if, I mused, this performance was not mere acting, but a veiled confession, a narrative concealing a darker truth? Surely, no ordinary man could stage such a play while Jack the Ripper stalked the streets, claiming his victims with impunity. Yet, I kept these unsettling thoughts to myself, my outward demeanour betraying nothing of my inner turmoil, only letting my amazement show in my eyes.

As the curtain fell, I joined Holmes to venture into the labyrinthine alleys of London, the darkness pressing in on me, amplifying my already heightened sense of dread.

Mansfield's chilling portrayal of Mr. Hyde lingered in my mind, a disquieting counterpoint to the grim task that lay ahead. From the Lyceum, we reached Whitechapel by cab in a matter of ten minutes, completing the remainder of our journey on foot. Holmes had selected a secluded street, one he believed Levy was likely to frequent. Earlier in the evening, we had determined our respective positions, strategically placed to intercept our quarry. We now dispersed, melting into the shadows, each of us isolated and unaware of the others' precise locations. We had no means of confirming our colleagues' deployments; we could only rely on trust and a shared understanding of the plan.

Concealed in the darkness and silence, my thoughts revolved around Jacob Levy, the man we believed to be the Whitechapel fiend. If, as Holmes suspected, he had contracted syphilis from the prostitutes he frequented, he certainly possessed a motive for these brutal attacks. He resided in the very heart of the murder district, and his butcher shop provided both a convenient location for cleansing himself after his gruesome deeds and a secure repository for his macabre trophies. His medical records attested to his mental instability, a consequence of the advanced stage of his disease. He was a Jewish businessman, skilled in the use of a knife, possessing a rudimentary understanding of anatomy. All the evidence, it seemed, pointed inexorably towards Jacob Levy's guilt. There could be no doubt, I thought, that we had finally identified the Whitechapel murderer.

Tonight, I thought, the world would finally learn the true identity of Jack the Ripper. The era of fear and speculation, fueled by sensationalist newspaper reports, would come to an end. The truth, at last, would be revealed.

The indiscriminate attribution of every unsolved murder to the mythical "Jack the Ripper" would cease. We would finally be able to determine whether these atrocities were the work of a single individual, or the product of multiple, independent acts of violence.

My thoughts raced, and I could feel the insistent thump of my own heart against my ribs.

Holmes and I were concealed behind a stack of crates and barrels at the end of a dimly lit street, mere moments away, we hoped, from concluding our pursuit of Jacob Levy. We knew that, once midnight had passed, the killer was likely to appear at any time between two and six o'clock in the morning.

Suddenly, around two o'clock, Holmes stiffened, his body rigid with anticipation. Knowing that he was alerted by the slightest sound or movement, I, too, strained my senses, listening intently. A moment later, I heard it – the unmistakable sound of approaching footsteps.

The silence of the night was broken by the slow, heavy tread. We pressed ourselves deeper into the shadows, our eyes fixed upon the darkened street.

The footsteps grew louder, closer. A chill wind swept down from the direction of Whitechapel Road, and I shivered involuntarily. Despite the knowledge that Abberline and his men were strategically positioned throughout the area, a prickle of fear ran down my spine. I gripped my revolver tightly, my finger hovering near the trigger, ready to act at a moment's notice.

Then, a figure emerged from the darkness, the silhouette of a man – the man we had been hunting relentlessly.

He materialised from the swirling mist, clad in a long coat, a hat pulled low over his face, obscuring his features. Holmes later confided that he had recognized Jacob Levy instantly by his distinctive gait – a peculiar swing in his step – and the aura of barely suppressed rage that seemed to emanate from him.

At Holmes's prearranged signal, I sprang from our hiding place, my revolver levelled at the approaching figure. The soldier in me, honed by the battles of the Afghan war, momentarily eclipsed the doctor and the writer.

"Jacob Levy!" I roared, my voice echoing through the deserted street. "You are under arrest for the murders of Mary Ann Nichols, Annie Chapman, Elizabeth Stride, Catherine Eddowes, and Mary Jane Kelly!"

But as I caught a glimpse of his face beneath the shadow of his hat, I froze. A primal urge to put a bullet through the head of this monster, this purveyor of terror, surged through me, yet my hand, gripping the revolver, felt strangely numb and unresponsive. A silent scream echoed in my mind; this was surely the devil incarnate, walking the streets of London in human guise.

He paused momentarily, his silence more menacing than any words. Then, seeing the fear etched upon my face, he erupted in a chilling, maniacal laughter.

Too late, I realised the truth of Holmes's earlier words; the police were not coming to my aid. Knowing that his game was up, Jacob Levy whipped a knife from his coat pocket with his left hand and lunged towards me, his teeth bared in a snarl of pure animalistic rage.

I squeezed the trigger repeatedly, but the revolver remained stubbornly silent. My fingers, numbed by the cold night air, refused to cooperate. I took a few steps back.

Just as Jacob Levy was upon me, poised to strike, Holmes launched himself from the shadows, delivering a powerful blow to the man's side, sending the knife flying from his grasp. Holmes struck again, a swift, precise chop to the back of Levy's neck. The man crumpled to the ground at my feet. In a flash, Holmes was upon him, pinning his arms behind his back, rendering him immobile. Sensation returned to my hand, and I pressed the muzzle of my revolver against Levy's temple.

The monster beneath me growled, his eyes burning with hatred.

I saw figures emerging from the darkness, converging upon us. For a moment, I imagined them to be the vengeful spirits of Levy's victims. But they were, in fact, Abberline and his men, rushing to our aid.

Holmes released Levy's arms and delivered one final blow to the back of his head. The man lay still, his struggles ceasing. I saw Holmes's eyes gleaming in the darkness, reflecting the gaslight that spilled into the alley.

As Levy lay there, momentarily subdued, Abberline's men swarmed over him, securing his wrists with handcuffs and pinning him to the ground. He thrashed and writhed, a caged animal in a frenzy of rage. A cloud of dust rose from the cobblestones, and the sounds of the struggle echoed briefly through the night before fading into silence. In the flickering gaslight, Holmes's face shone with triumph.

I breathed a sigh of relief, offering a grateful glance towards my friend. He stood over Jacob Levy, his gaze fixed upon the face of the man who had terrorised London for so long. The intensity of Holmes's gaze, I noted, far surpassed the malevolent glare of the captured killer.

The reign of terror wrought by Jack the Ripper had finally come to an end. London, at long last, could sleep soundly.

EPILOGUE

I.

Several years had elapsed since the horrors of that autumn, and at last, I had completed my chronicle of the Whitechapel atrocities, a volume I entitled The Autumn of Terror. I presented the manuscript to Holmes, who devoured its contents with his customary alacrity.

I confess, a certain pride swelled within me at the recollection of how my friend, Sherlock Holmes, had unraveled a mystery that had baffled even the most astute minds at Scotland Yard, including the redoubtable Frederick Abberline.

My narrative style, too, had evolved, thanks in no small part to Holmes's pointed critiques. "You owe me a debt of gratitude, Watson," he remarked, returning the manuscript, "for my criticisms, which have, I trust, rendered your prose somewhat more palatable." I could not suppress a smile; his praise, however grudgingly given, was music to my ears. Moreover, the prospect of revealing the identity of the Whitechapel fiend to the world at large filled me with a profound sense of satisfaction.

"I am undecided, Holmes," I ventured, "as to whether The Autumn of Terror or The Mystery of Whitechapel would be the more fitting title for this work."

He merely smiled enigmatically, offering no opinion on the matter.

"It is a profound relief, Holmes," I remarked, "to have finally brought this affair to a close. The killer, it must be said, possessed a remarkable cunning, a deep understanding of the criminal underworld of London. He proved a truly worthy adversary, even for you. Indeed, I might venture to suggest that, on this occasion, he very nearly outwitted you." I offered this observation in a spirit of genuine admiration, believing it would please my friend.

However, a shadow fell across his features, and I realised, with a sinking heart, that my final remark had struck a discordant note.

"Is that truly your assessment, Watson?" he inquired, his voice tight with displeasure. I was taken aback, rendered speechless by his unexpected reaction.

He rose abruptly and made to snatch the manuscript from my grasp. I clutched it protectively, like a miser guarding his gold. The fireplace, a mere few feet away, filled me with a sudden dread; I feared he might consign my hard work to the flames.

"I merely wish to highlight certain passages, Watson," he explained, his voice softening slightly, "that demonstrate the fallacy of your assertion. I implore you, be more analytical in your appraisal of your own work." He settled back into his chair, leaning towards me intently.

I held the manuscript close, my heart still pounding, and prepared to listen to his critique.

"Watson," Holmes began, his voice low and reproachful, "I never imagined you would take this…incomplete narrative, the details of which I withheld from you, and present it to the world. I fear it was not your literary aspirations, but rather your precarious financial situation, that motivated this undertaking." He gestured towards the manuscript with a disapproving frown.

"Incomplete narrative?" I echoed, surprised. Holmes's expression immediately registered a flicker of regret at having revealed so much.

"Very well," he sighed, waving a dismissive hand. "Do as you please. But I maintain that this work is not yet ready for publication." He fell silent, his brow furrowed in thought.

Seizing the opportunity presented by his silence, I replaced the manuscript upon the bookshelf. I sensed a deliberate attempt at distraction, yet Holmes remained lost in contemplation. I poured two glasses of brandy, offering one to my friend. He accepted the glass with a wan smile, taking a sip while his mind still wrestled with some unseen problem.

"I propose a compromise, Holmes," I suggested, an idea forming in my mind. "I shall revise the manuscript, rewriting it in the first person, as if narrated by yourself. This will offer the reader a fresh perspective. You may then supplement the narrative with any details you deem appropriate." I set my own glass aside and leaned against the wall, observing him closely.

"Good heavens, Watson, no!" Holmes exclaimed, his voice laced with alarm. "You would do better to publish it under Moriarty's name!" He drained his brandy glass in a single gulp, a gesture of agitation I had rarely witnessed. The Holmes I knew courted danger, rather than shrinking from it. This uncharacteristic display of apprehension was deeply unsettling. He fixed me with an intense stare.

"If I were to divulge certain sensitive information, Watson," he began, his voice low and confidential, "you would understand the reasons for my reticence." He gestured towards me with his empty glass, a silent request for more brandy. I obliged, refilling his glass and returning the decanter to the table before taking another sip from my own.

What could he possibly mean? I watched him over the rim of my glass, my curiosity piqued. This time, he seemed to savour the brandy, a flicker of his usual composure returning to his features.

"We apprehended the Whitechapel killer, the butcher Jacob Levy," I pointed out, summarising the known facts. "The court, deeming him insane, committed him to Stone Asylum. And with his confinement, the atrocities ceased. I understand that his syphilis progressed rapidly within the asylum walls, ultimately leading to his demise. A fitting end, I would say, for such a depraved individual. So, you speak of an incomplete narrative, Holmes. I confess, I fail to grasp your meaning."

"What truly transpired, my dear Watson," Holmes stated, his voice low and serious, "is far more complex than it appears on the surface." He looked down, a rare expression of helplessness flitting across his features.

"I believe we were manipulated, Watson, by a narrator far more skilled than yourself. He cleverly diverted our attention, painting a compelling, yet ultimately misleading, picture of the Whitechapel murders, leading us to perceive them as the work of a single individual. He successfully implanted the notion, both within the public consciousness and within our own minds, that all eleven murders were committed by one serial killer. I only later came to understand the intricacies of his deception."

"Of whom do you speak, Holmes?" I inquired, my curiosity piqued.

"Moriarty," he replied, his voice barely a whisper.

I could not recall any mention of Moriarty in connection with this case. "Moriarty?" I echoed, perplexed. "But how…?"

"Amongst the documents seized from Sebastian Moran's residence following his arrest," Holmes explained, "I discovered a letter penned by Moriarty himself. A document, I might add, that casts an entirely new light upon the Whitechapel affair." My curiosity intensified. "It was, in essence, a handbook, a guide to criminal enterprise, bequeathed by Moriarty to his protégé. Within its pages, he confesses to employing his unique talents to orchestrate certain…reenactments…in order to protect a client. I believe this slip of the tongue, this inadvertent revelation, stemmed from a desire for admiration, a need to impress his protégé and bolster his own ego. Moriarty, despite his intellect, was remarkably susceptible to flattery. It was praise, not power, that truly fueled his ambition, compelling him to boast of his cleverness."

I now understood the source of Holmes's frustration. "So, while the surface narrative appeared straightforward, Moriarty was working behind the scenes, manipulating events to elevate this case to a matter of international significance," Holmes added with a sigh, his shoulders slumping slightly.

"His intellect, had it been directed towards nobler pursuits, could have benefited mankind immeasurably," he lamented. His tone conveyed both respect for Moriarty's formidable mind and profound disappointment at its perversion.

"While I initially dismissed the case as relatively simple," he continued, "Moriarty's involvement introduced layers of complexity. In his handbook, he expresses a surprising degree of sympathy for the plight of London's prostitutes. This, I must say, is entirely out of character. From what I know of the man, he delighted in the moral decay of society. I encountered this sentiment myself in one of his letters." He referred to the document he had retrieved from Moran's residence. "This handbook, intended for Moran's eyes only, fell into the hands of the police upon his arrest. That arrest brought an end to Moriarty's network." Holmes retrieved a folded piece of paper from a file in his cabinet.

"Upon learning of the discovery of a document authored by Moriarty himself," Holmes explained, "I immediately requested that my contacts at Scotland Yard allow me to examine it. I even offered to take possession of it, as a…memento, a trophy commemorating the downfall of Moriarty's network. However, my request was denied. I managed to acquire only this single page. Had I obtained the entire handbook, it would have proved a most illuminating study in criminal methodology. It is likely languishing, unread, in some dusty archive at Scotland Yard." He sighed, a hint of frustration in his voice. "However," he continued, "in this fragment, Moriarty mentions his involvement in the Whitechapel investigation, at the invitation of Mr. Lusk."

"So," I exclaimed, the pieces of the puzzle falling into place, "he was the mysterious 'Le Grand'!"

"Precisely, Watson. Le Grand. 'The Skillful One.' 'The Professor.'"

Holmes handed me the page, and I began to read.

II.

'The killer departed the scene without making any attempt at concealment. I know that you, my dear reader, will find this puzzling, but I assure you, it was a calculated move, executed precisely as I instructed. To effectively misdirect one's pursuers, one must possess a deep understanding of the human psyche.'

'They were eager to deploy bloodhounds throughout Whitechapel. However, were the populace to learn that such a measure was being taken due to a complete lack of viable suspects, implying that anyone in the district could be the culprit, it would have undoubtedly incited widespread panic and unrest. I therefore concocted a narrative, a convenient scapegoat, to allay their fears and assure them that the search was focused upon a single individual. As I anticipated, the operation proceeded without incident, the public suitably pacified.'

'This afforded me an excellent opportunity to put into practice Machiavelli's principle of obscuring the truth by disseminating a carefully crafted narrative, thereby shaping public perception and diverting attention from the true nature of events.'

'Moreover, this "hunt," as it were, provided me with invaluable insights into the investigative methods of the police and, more importantly, how to circumvent them. The consultations I have conducted over the past few months are a testament to the efficacy of this strategy. I orchestrated these meetings precisely to gain access to their innermost deliberations.'

'I have been closely monitoring the various theories put forth by the police and Scotland Yard, gaining a thorough understanding of their deductive processes. These hypotheses ranged from the preposterous – a connection to the Freemasons, or the involvement of a local physician – to the truly absurd – the implication of a grandson of Queen Victoria herself!'

'The time has now come, however, to unveil the truth.'

'The element that so confounded detectives such as Sherlock Holmes was the conspicuous absence of any tangible evidence pointing towards a specific suspect. Holmes, as we know, relies heavily upon empirical observation to form his conclusions. A case such as this, devoid of such clues, left him floundering.'

'The foundation of law is justice and logic. Its pronouncements are based upon the available evidence. However, this very principle is also its Achilles' heel. Evidence can be manufactured. Public opinion can be manipulated. Logic can be twisted to serve one's own ends. One need only understand the when, the where, the how, and upon whom. Execute these elements flawlessly, and the process will unfold organically, gathering momentum like a boulder rolling down a hill. Our role is merely to apply the initial impetus, to nudge the boulder in the desired direction, then step aside and observe the ensuing chaos. The masses, fixated upon the devastating trajectory of the boulder, will never consider the hand that set it in motion.'

'I shall now elucidate how I employed my intellect not only to identify the true culprit, but also to exploit these murders to safeguard my client. As my client is now deceased, I am no longer bound by the constraints of professional discretion, and may therefore divulge the full extent of my machinations without fear of damaging his reputation.'

'Suffice it to say, I advised my client to emulate the methods of Jack the Ripper in order to evade capture. He sought my counsel after committing the murder and securing the premises. Having received my guidance, he departed. His identity, I believe, is of no relevance to this narrative.'

'You will have surmised, by now that my client risked attracting the attention of Scotland Yard by his overly zealous imitation of the Ripper's methods. Therefore, I shall refrain from providing a detailed description. He was, after all, merely a client. He listened impassively as I berated him for his foolish and unnecessary actions. He expressed gratitude that I was not affiliated with Scotland Yard – indeed, he offered fervent thanks to Providence for this fact – and, upon my advice, booked passage on a ship bound for South Africa the very next day, having first remunerated me thrice the agreed-upon sum.'

'I instructed him to remove certain organs from the body, including the uterus, the very essence of her womanhood. It mirrored the Ripper's signature mutilations. However, there remained a crucial discrepancy between the first four murders and this one. The initial killings, executed with a butcher's precision, led the police to suspect a professional hand. In contrast, the removal of organs in this instance, while extensive, lacked the same anatomical expertise, thereby confounding their attempts to identify a suspect.'

'My own insatiable curiosity, however, would not allow me to rest until I had unmasked the true killer, the real Jack the Ripper, not the mere imitator acting upon my instructions. I was determined to understand the depths of his depravity, the wellspring of his rage and fury. To achieve this, I embarked upon a meticulous reconstruction of the events leading up to the murders…'

III.

The page ended abruptly, leaving me hanging on a precipice of unanswered questions. I glanced at Holmes, wondering if he had, in fact, perused the entire handbook. The knowing glint in his eye and the subtle smile playing upon his lips confirmed my suspicions. This isolated fragment, divorced from its context, offered little in the way of concrete information. However, having read the complete text, I now understood why Holmes had surreptitiously removed this particular page from the clutches of Scotland Yard. It seemed that Moriarty, initially intent on unmasking the true killer, had ultimately exploited the opportunity to protect his client through a clever act of misdirection. Yet, the handbook also indicated that Moriarty had persisted in his pursuit of the real Ripper. Had he succeeded? And if so, who was the true culprit? My mind reeled with possibilities.

"What the handbook fails to mention, Watson," Holmes interjected, his voice low and thoughtful, "is that Lusk was manipulated into engaging Moriarty's services. Moriarty employed his network of agents to subtly guide Lusk towards him. Lusk would never have been able to contact Moriarty unless Moriarty himself desired it."

He paused, his eyes twinkling. "'Le Grand,'" he murmured, the name laced with irony. I nodded, acknowledging the deception.

I recalled Holmes's account of his protracted pursuit of Moriarty, a chase that had spanned years. Even Holmes, with his unparalleled deductive abilities, had found it remarkably difficult to penetrate the veil of secrecy surrounding the Professor's criminal empire. He had first encountered Moriarty face-to-face when the Professor, in a brazen display of audacity, had paid a visit to our Baker Street rooms, explicitly threatening Holmes. I, fortunately or unfortunately, had been absent on that memorable occasion.

Following this encounter, Holmes had orchestrated an elaborate scheme to ensnare Moriarty and his network, culminating in our dramatic flight across Europe. I knew that he had taken these drastic measures to protect both our lives. Reflecting upon these past events, I readily accepted Holmes's assertion regarding Moriarty's manipulation of Lusk.

He set his empty glass upon the table beside him.

"Had you read the complete handbook, Watson," he continued, "you would have observed how Moriarty boasts of solving the case through sheer intellect, rather than relying upon empirical evidence. He then proceeds to disseminate his carefully crafted narrative, instilling it within the public consciousness. He cunningly fostered the belief in a serial killer obsessed with collecting the uteri of his victims as trophies. Such behaviour, as you know, is highly unusual. Moriarty had a very specific reason for propagating this particular narrative."

He paused, his eyes narrowing. "Did you know, Watson that this same Moriarty, who lamented the widespread panic caused by the lurid newspaper accounts of the murders of prostitutes, hosted a lavish banquet for the editors of those very newspapers in early August of that year?"

"You mean, before the infamous five murders occurred?" I asked.

"Precisely," Holmes replied. It was clear he had uncovered a detail he wished to share.

"I am convinced that Moriarty clandestinely conspired with these editors, orchestrating a plan to divert public attention. This would have been prior to his manipulation of Lusk to suit his own ends. It's astonishing, Watson," Holmes mused, "that someone like Lusk could be ensnared in such a scheme."

Yet my mind wrestled with another question. "We've gathered substantial evidence identifying Jack the Ripper over the years. Why, then, do you urge me not to publish this?"

"This will only perpetuate the mystery, my friend," I argued. "Readers will eventually question my integrity for withholding this story, especially after such revelations. They'll wonder where the great detective Sherlock Holmes was during these dreadful events in London. If we don't disclose our findings, it could tarnish your reputation."

Holmes pondered this for a moment.

"Perhaps you are right, Watson," Holmes conceded. "However, publication could inflict far greater damage to our reputations."

"How so?" I inquired, puzzled.

"You yourself mentioned the numerous suspects who fit the Ripper profile. This is true. But to reveal this list publicly would be to invite unwanted scrutiny and entanglement in a most unpleasant affair. Do you recall a particular name on that list, one that caused you considerable consternation?"

I racked my brain, trying to recall the individual in question.

"Let me see…the Spitalfields pimps, Aaron Kosminski, Ludwig, and Jacob Levy," I recited, listing the names most frequently associated with the Whitechapel murders.

"Watson," Holmes said, his voice grave, his expression unusually sombre, "I believe you should sit down before you hear the rest." I had never seen him so serious. I quickly drained my glass and sat down in the chair he indicated.

"You will inevitably find discrepancies and inconsistencies in the accounts of these murders, Watson, no matter how diligently you scrutinise them," Holmes began, his voice low and intense. "I shall endeavour to explain these irregularities, clearly and concisely. However, I must warn you, the truth may prove unsettling. Once I have finished, the entire mystery will be laid bare, the gaps filled, the inconsistencies resolved. But be prepared, Watson, for a shock. When I have concluded, you will understand the reasons for my reticence."

He rose and closed the window, then opened the door and peered into the hallway, ensuring our privacy. He even went so far as to lock the door, a gesture that heightened my sense of unease.

"Holmes," I said, my voice barely above a whisper, "you are making me exceedingly nervous. Pray tell, what is this all about?"

Satisfied that we were alone, Holmes resumed his seat, leaning closer, his voice barely audible.

"You have omitted a crucial name from your list of suspects. Do you recall Moriarty's confession regarding a certain individual, a client whose identity he wished to protect, someone he deliberately shielded from the law?"

"Ah, yes!" I exclaimed, "The man he advised to flee to South Africa!"

Holmes raised a hand, silencing me.

"If this list were to include a member of the Royal Family, Watson," he murmured, his voice barely a whisper, "would you still be so eager to publish it?"

"Royalty?" I gasped, my mind reeling.

"Indeed, Watson," Holmes confirmed, his eyes fixed upon mine. "Prince Albert Victor."

IV.

His words struck me like a physical blow, leaving me breathless and disoriented.

Holmes waited patiently while I struggled to regain my composure, a process that took some considerable time.

A thousand questions clamoured for attention within my mind, yet I could articulate none of them. Holmes, sensing my confusion, resumed his narrative.

"A certain rumour, Watson, concerning a grandson of the Queen, circulated amongst the highest echelons of society. It was whispered in hushed tones within the hallowed halls of gentlemen's clubs, its details shrouded in secrecy. You, my dear fellow, would never have encountered such gossip."

"A rumour, you say?"

"The story went that Prince Albert Victor, disguised to avoid recognition, frequented the establishments of…unfortunate women. Some even claimed to have seen him in such compromising circumstances."

"In brothels?" I exclaimed, aghast. "That's unthinkable. Where was he allegedly seen?"

"In Whitechapel, Watson," Holmes replied, his voice grave. "The very district where these murders occurred."

The room seemed to spin around me, and a roaring filled my ears. I snatched the brandy decanter from the table, poured a generous measure into my glass, and swallowed it in a single gulp.

"Were these rumours true?" I asked, my voice barely a whisper.

"Good heavens, Watson, don't you see?" Holmes exclaimed. "The veracity of the rumours is irrelevant! These were allegations concerning the future King of England! The mere suggestion of such impropriety, true or not, would have had devastating consequences for the monarchy."

"Did the Queen know?"

"I cannot say for certain. But were such a story to appear in print, every anarchist and anti-royalist in the country would be up in arms."

"But they are merely rumours," I protested.

"We are speaking of the Queen's grandson, Watson! If he were indeed frequenting the lowliest dens of iniquity…" His voice trailed off, leaving the unspoken implications hanging heavy in the air.

"There's no proof, Holmes," I argued, "only conjecture."

"Conjecture?" Holmes retorted, his voice rising slightly. "The Whitechapel case was one of the most complex and perilous investigations we have ever undertaken. It involved the combined efforts of numerous experts, making it arguably the largest manhunt in British history. If the Prince were implicated in these atrocities, the very future of the monarchy would be jeopardised."

Prince Albert Victor, also the Duke of Clarence and Avondale, was the eldest son of the Prince and Princess of Wales. Despite being second in line to the throne, he never ascended to the titles of King or Prince of Wales, as he predeceased both his grandmother, Queen Victoria, and his father.

"He was known within the Royal Family as 'Eddie'," Holmes continued, his voice now low and measured. "Prince Eddie served as a naval cadet, travelling extensively. Upon reaching adulthood, he joined the army, though he never saw active service. After two failed romantic attachments, he became engaged to Princess Victoria of Teck. However, just weeks after the announcement of their betrothal, Prince Eddie died under…mysterious circumstances." His words hung in the air, heavy with unspoken implications. I could scarcely believe what I was hearing.

"Mysterious circumstances?" I echoed, my voice hushed. "He succumbed to influenza during the pandemic. The Princess subsequently married his younger brother." I, too, adopted a more cautious tone, sensing the delicate nature of this revelation. Yet, I still struggled to comprehend Holmes's implications.

"Albert Victor's intellect, his sexuality, and indeed, his psychological well-being, were the subject of much speculation," Holmes continued. "You may recall his name being mentioned in connection with the Cleveland Street scandal, involving a male brothel."

"And our friend, Frederick Abberline," he added, "the officer in charge of the Whitechapel investigation, was also involved in the Cleveland Street affair. He was deeply disillusioned by the police force's handling of the matter, recognizing the deliberate suppression of certain inconvenient truths. This disillusionment ultimately led to his retirement from the service."

"I remember the scandal well," I replied. "However, there was no concrete evidence linking the Prince to that establishment. Nor was there any proof of his alleged homosexuality. In fact, there's no definitive evidence placing him in London during the Whitechapel murders." My memory, now fully engaged, supplied these pertinent details.

Holmes, however, seemed determined to present his case as if I were entirely ignorant of the Prince's history, and continued his exposition.

"He was christened Albert Victor Christian Edward by the Archbishop of Canterbury," Holmes stated, "but was known affectionately as 'Eddie' within the Royal Family. The name Victor was chosen in honour of his grandmother, Queen Victoria, and her late husband, Albert. As the eldest son of the Prince of Wales, he was heir presumptive to the throne. He spoke his mother's native Danish fluently, but displayed little aptitude for other languages or academic pursuits. His tutors described him as a slow learner, with a marked inability to concentrate."

"Holmes," I interrupted, a sudden thought striking me, "the letters intended to implicate the Jewish community contained numerous grammatical errors. Could they have been written by someone like the Prince, someone with limited linguistic skills?"

"Possibly," Holmes replied, choosing his words carefully. "Someone of similar educational background. Witnesses also reported that the killer spoke with a foreign accent. The Prince's fluency in Danish, and his lack of proficiency in other languages, could certainly account for this."

"Good heavens, Holmes!" I exclaimed, the implications of his words sinking in. But the weariness in his eyes told me that he had borne this knowledge for some time. He continued his explanation, his voice heavy with the weight of the secret he had carried for so long.

"It is believed that he inherited his mother's predisposition to deafness," Holmes explained, "which may have contributed to his…intellectual challenges. His lack of focus, his disruptive behaviour in the classroom, and his general academic struggles could all be attributed to this underlying condition. He was subsequently enrolled in the Royal Naval College, as a naval cadet. By the age of sixteen, he was a midshipman, and embarked on a series of voyages throughout the British Empire, visiting America, the Falkland Islands, Australia, Fiji, South Africa, India, Ceylon, Singapore, Aden, Egypt, the Holy Land, Greece, and even acquiring a tattoo in Japan. He returned to England at the age of eighteen."

"It was shortly after his return," Holmes continued, his voice dropping to a conspiratorial whisper, "that the Whitechapel murders began. I need not recount the details of those horrors; they are etched indelibly upon our memories."

"However, it was after the Ripper murders that the Cleveland Street scandal erupted. Do you recall the police raid on a male brothel operated by one Charles Hammond in 1889? Those involved were sentenced to two years' hard labour for their unconventional activities."

"This particular incident sent shockwaves through the upper echelons of British society," Holmes explained, "due to rumours of a royal connection. The individual implicated, Watson, was none other than Prince Albert Victor." He leaned back in his chair, steepling his fingers, and fixed me with a knowing gaze.

"However," I countered, "none of the prostitutes involved mentioned Prince Albert Victor by name. I believe the rumours originated with Arthur Somerset's lawyer, a deliberate attempt to deflect attention from his client."

"Let me tell you how the story truly unfolded, Watson," Holmes said, a glint in his eye. "It's a rather fascinating tale. The police were questioning a telegraph boy found in possession of a suspiciously large sum of money. As you know, such lads are not typically well-remunerated. The boy initially claimed that the money represented his savings. However, under persistent questioning, he confessed, revealing the names of several male prostitutes, their pimps, and, most importantly, their clients. Amongst these names were some of the most prominent figures in British society, including that of Lord Arthur Somerset, an equerry to the Prince of Wales. Yet, the police released him without charge. When pressed to identify the individual financing these activities, he offered only three initials."

"Three initials?"

"Indeed, Watson. P.A.V."

"Prince Albert Victor," I murmured.

V.

"I made discreet inquiries into this matter," Holmes continued, his voice low and conspiratorial. "I discovered that in December of 1889, the Prince received a series of anonymous letters, threatening in nature. I was unable to ascertain the identity of the sender, but I strongly suspect the hand of Moriarty. He likely used these letters to blackmail the Prince, coercing him into compliance in exchange for his silence. However, I found no concrete evidence linking the Prince to any of these incidents. There was nothing to substantiate the rumours of his involvement with male brothels."

"Are you suggesting, then," I asked, "that the rumours were entirely fabricated?" Holmes remained silent, his expression unreadable. "If he were indeed homosexual in 1889, how could he possibly be the Ripper, the man who brutally murdered five women in 1888?"

"Precisely," Holmes said, a slow smile spreading across his face. He had been waiting for me to reach this conclusion on my own.

"So that was the purpose of the rumours!" I exclaimed. "If everyone suspected him of the Ripper murders, as I did, they would naturally dismiss any other…irregularities in his behaviour."

"But why," I asked, "was there no mention of Prince Albert Victor in the newspapers? Not even a whisper of his name?"

"The press was silenced, Watson," Holmes replied. "Moriarty, I believe, ensured that Albert Victor's name never appeared in print. One particularly tenacious investigative journalist was even dismissed from his post during this period. He later claimed to have received threats, and hinted at a conspiracy within the Secret Service to spread rumours about a member of the Royal Family. He was warned that his newspaper would be shut down if he published anything without irrefutable proof, and he himself faced the threat of imprisonment."

"However, Watson," Holmes continued, "while the British press remained silent, the American newspapers were not so easily intimidated. The New York Times described the Prince as a 'dullard,' a 'stupid perverse boy,' and declared that he should 'never be permitted to ascend the British throne.'"

"In the autumn of 1889, Albert Victor embarked on a tour of India," Holmes continued. "The American press speculated that he was attempting to escape the scandal and repair his damaged reputation. However, my investigations revealed that the trip had been planned since the summer. He travelled to Bombay via Athens, Port Said, Cairo, and Aden, spending much of his time…'hunting,' as he called it." He winked, a sardonic glint in his eye.

"So the Autumn of Terror," I remarked dryly, "shifted to India." Holmes nodded in agreement.

"It was during this tour that Albert Victor became acquainted with Margery Haddon, the wife of Henry Haddon, a civil engineer. Following Albert Victor's untimely death, Mrs. Haddon arrived in England, claiming that he was the father of her son, Clarence

Haddon. She was, I understand, rather given to intemperance. News of her allegations reached Buckingham Palace, prompting an investigation by the Special Branch. I examined their files, but found nothing of substance. Mrs. Haddon possessed no evidence to support her claims. However, I did discover a rather intriguing detail – Albert Victor's lawyers acknowledged a 'relationship' between the Prince and Mrs. Haddon, but vehemently denied his paternity of the child."

"That child," I remarked, "could one day attempt to claim the throne."

"He would face considerable opposition from the Royal Family," Holmes replied. "It would be a difficult, if not impossible, task. Besides, an illegitimate child, regardless of the veracity of Mrs. Haddon's claims, cannot inherit the crown. The line of succession is clearly defined."

"Nevertheless," I countered, "the reputation of the Royal Family would suffer irreparable damage."

"Buckingham Palace," Holmes said with a sigh, "has its own methods of managing such unpleasantness." He paused, then resumed his narrative. "The Prince returned from India for Queen Victoria's seventy-first birthday celebrations. He was subsequently created Duke of Clarence and Avondale in May of 1890."

"Did the Queen know about any of this?" I asked, but Holmes remained silent, his expression unreadable.

"In 1889," Holmes continued, "Queen Victoria proposed a match between Prince Albert Victor and his cousin, Princess Alix of Hesse. The Prince duly proposed to her at Balmoral, but she refused him."

"What woman in her right mind would reject the opportunity to become Queen of England?" I exclaimed, incredulous.

"She must have had her reasons, Watson," Holmes replied. "As his cousin, she would have been privy to information unavailable to the general public. For instance, the Prince had been consulting various physicians regarding a social disease. It was during this period that he fell gravely ill during the influenza pandemic. He was only twenty-eight years old when he died."

"His death paved the way for his younger brother, George, to ascend the throne," I observed.

"One might question, Watson," Holmes said, his voice low and ominous, "whether this was a matter of fortune, or a carefully orchestrated design." His words sent a shiver down my spine.

"The Royal Family," Holmes continued, "would have been understandably apprehensive about the prospect of someone with Albert Victor's limitations ascending the throne. I have also heard whispers that the true cause of his death was not influenza, but syphilis."

"Another rumour," he added, "suggests that he was pushed from a balcony on the orders of Lord Randolph Churchill, as part of a conspiracy to prevent him from becoming King."

"Did you investigate these claims, Holmes?"

"No, Watson. I believe Albert Victor's death was 'an act of providence,' shall we say, 'executed with foresight and a certain pragmatic ruthlessness.' It is not our place to question the workings of fate, which, in this instance, removed an unsuitable heir and cleared the path for the more capable Prince George."

"Prince Albert Victor," Holmes mused, "grandson of Queen Victoria, second in line to the throne of England. He was born to a life of privilege and ease, destined to rule. Yet fate, in its capricious cruelty, decreed otherwise. He gained a reputation for indolence and a certain lack of moral fibre. Then came the whispers of homosexuality, and the shadow of the Cleveland Street scandal. All this by 1892, when he was but twenty-eight years of age." He leaned back in his chair, his expression a mixture of sadness and resignation.

"So, you believe he did frequent male brothels?" I asked.

"He was not homosexual, Watson," Holmes replied firmly. "Don't you see? It was a carefully constructed fabrication, a smokescreen to conceal his predilection for female companionship, and, more importantly, his connection to the Whitechapel murders."

"But who would concoct such a story?"

Holmes paused, his eyes closing as he gathered his thoughts, his fingers steepled beneath his chin.

"You are not the only one with a talent for narrative, Watson," he said, opening his eyes and fixing me with a knowing gaze. "You yourself read a certain confession, an account of how one fabricated a story to avert public unrest during the bloodhound operation."

"Moriarty!" I exclaimed, the realisation dawning upon me.

"Do you now understand, Watson, that there might be another explanation, a completely different interpretation, for the missing 'trophies'?"

"You mean…the Prince's…" My voice trailed off, unable to articulate the horrific thought that had taken root in my mind. "Are you suggesting that…?"

"I am not stating anything definitively, Watson," Holmes cautioned. "This is merely a hypothesis, a conjecture. I lack the concrete evidence to prove it. It remains, for now, an assumption." He seemed reluctant to commit himself fully to such a scandalous accusation.

"We are forced, in the absence of conclusive proof, to rely upon conjecture," he continued. "Let me be clear, Watson. Based on the available evidence, we can deduce certain probabilities. By carefully selecting and analysing these probabilities, and comparing them with the known circumstances, we can arrive at a reasonable approximation of the truth. Given the foundation upon which these assumptions rest, I believe the following scenario is the most likely explanation for the events in question."

"And what is that, Holmes?" I pressed, eager to hear his theory articulated in full. I wanted to hear him say it, to give voice to the unspeakable suspicion that hung heavy in the air between us.

Holmes drew a long, slow breath, his gaze fixed upon me as he marshalled his thoughts.

"A woman in Whitechapel," he began, his voice low and measured, "finds herself with child. The father, I believe, is Prince Albert Victor. He, or perhaps a group of highly placed individuals acting on his behalf, conspire to dispose of the woman and her inconvenient offspring. They enlist Moriarty's expertise in orchestrating the murder."

"To deflect attention from this crime," he continued, "they fabricate a serial killer, a phantom menace stalking the streets of Whitechapel. This notion is reinforced by the numerous, and often lurid, newspaper reports circulating at the time. Indeed, it is possible that these very reports were funded and orchestrated for this specific purpose. We know that the editors and proprietors of various newspapers attended a lavish banquet some six months prior to the murders. While I have been unable to identify the individual who financed this gathering, it is clear that Moriarty was the mastermind behind it. He certainly would not have expended his own funds on such an enterprise."

As I grappled with the implications of Holmes's theory, he continued his narrative.

"Amidst this carefully orchestrated chaos, the pregnant woman is murdered. The removal of her uterus effectively disguises the true nature of the crime, making it appear to be another Ripper killing. The detectives, the police, the public…all are completely misled, and the truth remains hidden."

"You speak with such conviction, Holmes," I remarked, "as if you were an eyewitness to these events."

"Indeed, Watson," he replied, a wry smile playing on his lips. "However, I must reiterate that this is merely conjecture. I have no concrete evidence to support this hypothesis. In fact, there is evidence to suggest that Albert Victor was not the Ripper, and that the murders were committed by someone else entirely."

"And what, pray tell, is this evidence?" I inquired, my curiosity piqued.

"Consider, for instance, the night of the double murder – the thirtieth of September, 1888," Holmes began. "On that night, while Elizabeth Stride and Catherine Eddowes were being brutally murdered in Whitechapel, Albert Victor was at Balmoral, the Royal Family's Scottish retreat, some five hundred miles away. He was in attendance, along with Queen Victoria and other members of the Royal Family, at a gathering hosted for visiting German royalty. Royal records, family diaries, personal correspondence, newspaper reports, and eyewitness accounts all place him firmly at Balmoral on that night, far from the scene of the crimes."

"But what of the two murders that preceded the double event?" I asked. "Or the fifth murder?" Holmes chose not to address these questions directly.

"Let me put it this way, Watson," he continued. "Despite being born into a life of privilege and luxury, surrounded by wealth and comfort, Prince Albert Victor sought something more."

He paused, leaving me hanging on his words, and I waited patiently for him to elaborate.

"He craved blood, Watson!" Holmes exclaimed, his voice rising unexpectedly.

It was clear that his inherent loyalty to the Crown made it difficult for him to utter words that would tarnish the image of the monarchy. The words that would condemn a prince of the realm seemed to catch in his throat.

"Are you saying, Holmes," I asked, "that Prince Albert Victor was directly involved in the murders that terrorised London a few years ago?"

"I am not saying he was definitely involved, Watson," Holmes replied carefully. "I am saying that he could have been."

"That is a most serious accusation, Holmes," I said, rising to my feet, my mind in turmoil.

I paced before the fireplace, attempting to quell the disquiet that churned within me. Holmes watched me silently, his expression unreadable.

"This, Watson," he said, his voice low and earnest, "is precisely why I advise against publishing your account of the Whitechapel murders. I implore you, reconsider." His tone was almost pleading.

VI.

"I believe I have now ascertained the true perpetrator of each of the Whitechapel murders," Holmes declared, his voice regaining some of its customary assurance. "However, Moriarty's handbook suggests that Jacob Levy was not responsible for the murder of Mary Kelly in November."

"Unlike the other victims," he continued, "Kelly was young and relatively attractive. She was not murdered in the street, but within the confines of her own lodgings, a single room she occupied alone." He emphasised this point, as if it held particular significance.

"I have never witnessed a more gruesome spectacle than the scene at Miller's Court, Watson," he shuddered, the memory clearly still vivid in his mind. "The extent of the mutilation…even her own mother would not have recognized her. Her entrails were strewn about the room. Her uterus was missing, as was her heart. The sheer ferocity of the attack far surpassed the brutality of Levy's crimes. Such unrestrained savagery suggests the unbridled passion of a young man, a prince of the realm, rather than the calculated butchery of a middle-aged butcher like Levy."

His words were shocking, almost blasphemous.

I recalled Moriarty's description of the murder, and a chilling certainty settled upon me. It was the Prince, I thought, not Levy, who had committed this final, horrific act.

To publish Holmes's shocking assertion, linking Prince Albert Victor to these gruesome murders, would be an act of treason. I had no desire to incur the wrath of the Crown.

Holmes had stopped short of explicitly accusing the Prince of the other murders, merely suggesting his possible involvement. However, in the case of Mary Kelly, his implication was clear; he believed the Prince to be the killer.

"What are you saying, Holmes?" I asked, hoping for clarification.

"It is not I who makes this accusation, Watson," Holmes replied. "It is Moriarty. I am merely presenting his theory."

"But where is the proof?" I pressed.

"In Moriarty's own words," Holmes said, gesturing towards the page from the handbook.

"But the handbook doesn't mention the Prince by name," I countered.

"True," Holmes conceded, "but it strongly implies his involvement. The real evidence, however, lies in the medical records of Sir William Gull, the Prince's physician."

"And what do these records reveal?"

"According to Dr. Gull's notes, the Prince contracted syphilis during his time in the West Indies. The disease, Gull writes, resulted in a marked decline in the Prince's mental faculties.

Furthermore, in a letter written by the Prince himself, he describes experiencing the unpleasant symptoms of the disease."

"Who would disclose such personal details in a letter?" I asked, incredulous.

"This particular letter was addressed to Dr. Roche, another physician who had examined him. The Prince consulted numerous doctors regarding his condition. He describes, in graphic detail, the discharge he was experiencing, from his private parts. I saw the letter myself, Watson, and the handwriting is unmistakably his," Holmes stated with absolute certainty.

As a physician, I knew that such a symptom was indeed indicative of syphilis. A wave of despair washed over me.

"It is my belief, Watson," Holmes declared, his voice low and intense, "that this disease ravaged his mind, driving him to madness. And in his madness, he became Jack the Ripper, unleashing his fury upon the unfortunate women of Whitechapel. I am convinced that the Royal Family was aware not only of his deteriorating mental state, but also of his extracurricular activities."

As a physician, I knew that syphilis could indeed lead to insanity, and that the disease, in its advanced stages, was incurable, its progression marked by escalating madness and, ultimately, death.

"But why," I asked, "did they take no action to prevent these atrocities?"

"They did take action, Watson," Holmes replied. "They concealed the truth."

"Concealed it?" I echoed, incredulous.

"Do you remember the very first murder we investigated?"

"Of course," I replied. "The Buck's Row victim, Mary Ann Nichols."

"We found considerable evidence to suggest that the murder had not taken place at that location. The body had clearly been moved. And do you recall our puzzlement at the lack of blood at the scene?"

Indeed, I remembered this perplexing detail.

I now understood the implications of Holmes's theory. If he was correct, it would explain every inexplicable detail, every loose end of the Whitechapel mystery.

"Was it not the duty of the Royal Family," I asked, "to at least attempt to control the Prince's wanderings?"

"They did, Watson," Holmes replied, "but only after the night of the double murder."

"What makes you say that?"

"Because following those two gruesome killings, there were no further murders until November."

"Good heavens!" I exclaimed, the pieces of the puzzle falling into place with chilling precision.

"And did you hear the rumours, Watson," Holmes continued, "of a black carriage, drawn by two magnificent black stallions, seen patrolling the streets of Whitechapel at night? A carriage bearing the Royal Crest."

"Why only rumours?" I asked.

"Do you imagine, Watson that any subject of this vast Empire, upon which the sun never sets, would dare to openly accuse a member of the Royal Family of such indiscretions?" Holmes countered. "It is said that those who witnessed the carriage remained silent, and even the police looked the other way."

"My God!" I murmured, my mind reeling.

"The November murder, that of Mary Kelly," Holmes continued, "was particularly brutal. It was this final atrocity, I believe, that finally convinced the Royal Family that the Prince's activities could no longer be tolerated. They were forced to act, to contain the damage. This, I believe, led to the orchestration of several subsequent murders, designed to mimic the Ripper's methods. The killings after November, in my opinion, were not committed by the Prince. They were staged to further confuse and misdirect the investigation."

"Apparently," he added, lowering his voice, "a rumour was circulated amongst the upper classes that Dr. Gull himself was seen driving the black carriage, luring prostitutes into it, and disposing of them within its confines."

"Preposterous!" I exclaimed. "Dr. Gull is a man of impeccable reputation, the Queen's own physician! Are you suggesting that he was the murderer?"

"I make no such accusation, Watson," Holmes replied calmly. "However, he is a physician, as you pointed out. He possesses the anatomical knowledge and surgical skill required to dissect a body and remove organs. Furthermore, attempting to mutilate a victim within a moving carriage would inevitably result in jagged, uneven incisions. This very irregularity was observed in the later victims. And the absence of blood at the scenes…well, the blood would naturally be contained within the carriage, the true location of the murders, not where the bodies were subsequently deposited. The murders, committed within the privacy of the carriage, would have no witnesses. And who would dare to report seeing a carriage bearing the Royal Crest in such suspicious circumstances?"

"Sir William Gull," I murmured, my mind reeling.

"However, Watson," Holmes continued, "I have several reasons to discount him as a suspect."

"And what are they?" I asked, eager to hear his reasoning.

"While Dr. Gull possessed the necessary skills and knowledge," Holmes explained, "he was, after all, merely a physician. He could not expect the same protection afforded to a member of the Royal

206

Family. While witnesses may have remained silent due to a failure to recognise him, I believe his involvement is highly improbable."

"Why is that, Holmes?"

"At the time of the murders, Dr. Gull was seventy-one years old and partially paralysed. He was simply not physically capable of committing such acts, regardless of his reputation or any mental instability he may have suffered."

"But if not Dr. Gull…" I stammered, my mind racing. "This case is a tangled web indeed. What of Jacob Levy? And how did the Prince acquire the anatomical knowledge to remove a uterus? This case is fraught with complexities."

"Syphilis, as you know, can lead to severe mental deterioration. The Prince's condition worsened considerably in his final years, and he was, in fact, confined to an asylum during his last days." Holmes's voice softened, as if reluctant to speak ill of the dead. "However, Watson," he continued, "considering all the suspects and the nature of the murders, there remains one glaring inconsistency. Do you know what it is?"

"We have yet to establish a motive, Holmes," I replied. "The why. We have been unable to determine a compelling reason for any of these suspects to commit such horrific crimes."

"Precisely, Watson," Holmes said, his voice taking on a new intensity. "The why. To explain my theory, I must first lay the groundwork, shall we say. But once I have done so, you will see that this crucial element of the mystery, the missing motive, will finally be revealed. I believe, Watson, that there was a very specific, and indeed, logical, reason for these murders."

I leaned forward, my curiosity now at fever pitch.

"My hypothesis, Watson," Holmes began, his voice low and conspiratorial, "is that one of these women, one of the victims of the Whitechapel murderer, was with child, fathered by Prince Albert Victor. To silence her, and to protect the reputation of the Royal Family, Moriarty concocted the persona of Jack the Ripper.

A single murder would have inevitably attracted unwanted scrutiny. Therefore, he orchestrated a series of killings, creating a climate of fear and confusion that obscured the true motive behind the crimes. And it was not only the woman herself who was silenced, Watson. Her friends, those who shared her secret, were also eliminated. These women, I believe, were all associates of Mary Jane Kelly. The entire plot, from beginning to end, was masterminded by Moriarty."

"This explains why some of the women were reluctant to identify themselves as Kelly's friends," I remarked, my mind racing. "They feared a similar fate."

"The removal of the uteri, then," I exclaimed, a sudden realisation dawning upon me, "was not the act of a depraved fetishist collecting trophies, but a deliberate attempt to destroy evidence!"

"Precisely, Watson," Holmes said, his voice ringing with triumph. "Had the uteri remained intact, the post-mortem examinations would have revealed that at least one of the victims was pregnant. Therefore, they created a fictional killer, a monster who mutilated his victims and removed their wombs. Under this guise, they removed the uterus of the woman they wished to silence, ensuring that Mary Kelly's murder appeared consistent with the others, and did not arouse suspicion."

The weight of these revelations pressed down upon me, almost too much to bear. I longed for the simpler narrative, the one in which Jacob Levy was the sole perpetrator, the one that offered a neat and tidy resolution to the Whitechapel horrors. Yet, Holmes's theory, as outlandish as it seemed, possessed a chilling logic. It was far more plausible that a series of murders had been orchestrated to conceal a single, scandalous pregnancy, than that a deranged butcher had been collecting uteri as souvenirs.

We now possessed a solution that connected all the disparate threads of the Whitechapel mystery. But the truth, it seemed, was far more terrible than we could have imagined.

"So, Jacob Levy, the butcher, committed these atrocities on behalf of the Prince, acting upon Moriarty's instructions," I summarised, my voice heavy with the weight of this terrible truth.

Holmes remained silent, his expression distant and detached. He methodically filled his pipe, a familiar gesture that, in this instance, seemed to emphasise his emotional removal from the horrors we had been discussing.

After a moment, he spoke, his voice low and thoughtful. "There is an inescapable truth, Watson that governs the workings of this world. You, I, the society in which we move, even the unfortunate women who sell their bodies for a pittance...we are all pawns in a larger game. Every single one of us. And it is the kings and queens, Watson, who dictate the moves, who determine the outcome. You should have realised this by now." His words held a deeper meaning, a veiled allusion I could not quite grasp. My mind, however, conjured an image of a chessboard, its pieces moving in accordance with some unseen hand.

I gazed at the manuscript, the culmination of countless hours of painstaking work, each detail meticulously recorded. A strange feeling washed over me, a sense that I had been...guided, compelled by some unseen force to chronicle the events of that Autumn of Terror.

"Was this entire affair," I asked, gesturing towards it, "a carefully orchestrated charade? A performance designed to mislead us, to incriminate Jacob Levy and protect the Prince?" My voice trembled with the enormity of the question.

Holmes, in response, silently placed his pipe between his lips and applied a match to the bowl.

"I find it difficult to believe that the Prince himself performed the...dissections," I remarked, my voice still tinged with disbelief.

Holmes took several long puffs from his pipe, his eyes closed, as if seeking solace in the familiar ritual.

"These are merely my deductions, Watson," he said, his voice calm and measured. "They are based on conjecture, not concrete evidence. And even if we did possess irrefutable proof, there is little we could do." He closed his eyes again, his face a mask of weariness.

"But these are not simply idle rumours, Holmes," I argued. "What if they prove to be true?"

"If the Prince frequented brothels," Holmes replied, his eyes opening, a steely glint in their depths. "It would be a scandal, certainly. But such scandals, however salacious, tend to fade with time, buried beneath the weight of more pressing matters. However, were the Prince to be accused of murder...that, my dear Watson, would shake the very foundations of the British Empire."

"The rumours, however outlandish," Holmes mused, "gain a certain credence when one considers the ineptitude displayed by the police during the Whitechapel investigation. They seemed to be operating without direction, like ships adrift without a rudder. I believe they were compelled to act against their better judgement, to overlook certain inconvenient truths." I recalled the sudden resignation of Sir Charles Warren, the Commissioner of the Metropolitan Police, immediately following the discovery of Mary Kelly's mutilated body on the ninth of November.

"Did you not sense it yourself, Watson?" Holmes asked, his voice low and intense. "That same feeling Abberline described, that there was something...amiss...some crucial piece of information being withheld from us? And that the individual, or individuals, responsible possessed the power to silence anyone who dared to speak out? Who else could order the Commissioner of Police from his bed in the middle of the night to remove bodies and destroy evidence?"

"Abberline did mention," I recalled, "that the Commissioner had already arrived at Mitre Square and removed Eddowes's body before he himself reached the scene. He had even erased the graffiti from the wall. I am now convinced that the Commissioner was acting under orders from the very highest levels of government, compelled to wander the streets in the dead of night, obliterating evidence."

VII.

A heavy silence descended upon the room, the weight of our deductions pressing down upon us. We sat there, two small figures dwarfed by the enormity of the truth we had uncovered, a truth too terrible to contemplate.

"So," I finally whispered, the words catching in my throat, "are you saying that Prince Albert Victor…was…Jack the Ripper?" The question, unspoken until now, hung heavy in the air between us.

"We shall likely never know the true identity of Jack the Ripper, Watson," Holmes replied, his voice heavy with resignation. He opened his eyes and glanced around the room, as if momentarily disoriented. "There is compelling evidence to suggest that several of the murders were committed by different individuals. This, I believe, was a deliberate strategy to deflect suspicion from the Prince."

"So you are saying," I clarified, "that the crimes attributed to Jack the Ripper were not the work of a single individual?"

"Precisely," Holmes affirmed.

"Therefore," I continued, "we cannot definitively conclude that Prince Albert Victor was Jack the Ripper, or even that he was directly involved in the murders, based solely on conjecture and the dubious testimony of a master manipulator like Moriarty."

"Indeed, Watson," Holmes agreed. "There is no irrefutable evidence to support such a claim." He closed his eyes again, taking a long, slow draw from his pipe, the smoke curling around his head like a shroud.

Holmes rose and, ignoring the brandy decanter, opened the cupboard behind it. He retrieved a bottle of Russian vodka, a rare indulgence he usually reserved for special occasions.

"Do you agree, Watson," he mused, as he poured two generous measures, "That knowledge can sometimes be a burden? Particularly the knowledge of unpleasant truths, truths that others remain blissfully unaware of? There is wisdom in the old adage, 'Ignorance is bliss.'"

"Consider, for instance, the theories of our esteemed colleague, Charles Darwin," he continued. "His observations are undeniably sound. Yet, millions still cling to the belief that mankind sprang from a naked couple residing in the Garden of Eden, tempted by the forbidden fruit. Try mentioning Mr. Darwin's name to a devout churchgoer, and observe the reaction."

"Let this story rest, Watson. We are chasing phantoms. You will find other, more palatable, narratives to pursue. Let us enjoy a glass of vodka, and clear our minds of these unpleasantries. I shall ask Mrs. Hudson to prepare us some bacon and eggs." He set the bottle and two glasses upon the table before me, then opened the door and called down the stairs to Mrs. Hudson, relaying our order. He returned, a more relaxed expression on his face, the tension of the past few hours seemingly dissipated.

He resumed his seat, avoiding my gaze as he poured a generous measure of vodka into each glass. He raised his glass in a silent toast, and I reciprocated.

"My dear Watson," he said, his voice tinged with a weary sadness, "it seems this case has led us into a labyrinth of dead ends and unanswered questions. Let us pursue it no further. We have borne the weight of this mystery for far too long. It is time to lay it aside, and find solace in the simpler pleasures of life. Let the world's mysteries rest for a while, Watson, and allow us to enjoy the bare necessities." He took a long draught of vodka, and I followed suit, the fiery liquid warming my throat and, momentarily, dispelling the chill that had settled upon my soul.

The End.

Made in the USA
Columbia, SC
17 November 2024

46780838R00117